The Dream Catcher

Annette Mori

The Dream Catcher

Annette Mori

Affinity
Rainbow Publications

2018

The Dream Catcher
© 2018 by Annette Mori

Affinity E-Book Press NZ LTD
Canterbury, New Zealand

1st Edition

ISBN: 978-1-98-854950-7

This is a work of fiction. Names, character, places, and incidents are the product of the author's imagination or are used fictitiously and any resemblance to actual persons living or dead, businesses, companies, events, or locales is entirely coincidental

Editor: Raven's Eye Editing, CK King
Proof Editor: Alexis Smith
Cover Design: Irish Dragon Design
Production Design: Affinity Publication Services

ACKNOWLEDGMENTS

A huge thank you to all of my beta readers: Gail Dodge, Cathie Williamson, Ali Spooner, Carrie Camp, Ameliah Faith, Dana Holmes, and Elle Hyden, who made great suggestions to improve the initial draft. Of course, once again, I have to acknowledge Erin O'Reilly, who is a constant support and encouragement to me. I am honored to call her a friend and to have her support me in my journey. I would also like to express my gratitude to Affinity Rainbow Publications and the wonderful trio (JM Dragon, Erin O'Reilly, and Nancy Kaufman) who continue to provide feedback to tighten up manuscripts that need assistance and publish my unconventional work. My other family members who are also very supportive, include my nephew, Aaron and his wife, Chelsea, my older sister and my father who struggles to read my books with one eye. I always enjoy working with the beta editor, Nancy Kaufman, who is so skilled at finding plot holes. Thanks to CK King for her magic as the final editor. She is a joy to work with. Inevitably, there are those pesky final errors that slip through, and I am thankful for the final proof editor, Alexis Smith, who catches those before the book goes to print. Thanks to Nancy Kaufman for the final cover. Nancy is also a promoter extraordinaire. A huge thanks to all the other readers and fellow writers who have sent personal e-mails, written reviews, and posted nice things on Facebook (you know who you are). The Affinity authors are an especially supportive group and often share posts or send words of encouragement. Finally, my wife, Jody, continues her support even when it interferes with our time together on the weekends.

DEDICATION

To the men and women who struggle with bipolar disorder, may their special gifts remain intact. To my wife, who is a constant support.

Table of Contents

PROLOGUE

I was the only one in the infirmary and that was fine with me. I never knew when I would slip into that dark place and put others in grave danger. Syl had been giving me medication to help me sleep and control my dreams. I wasn't particularly happy with the side effects, because it turned me into a zombie—alive but not really. And yet, it was better than the previous six months and Spartan's increasingly unbearable training.

Someone shook my shoulder and I popped open my eyes. Something was different. I felt clear headed when Syl shoved a set of clothes into my hands. "Put these on and get dressed."

I looked at her, wondering what was going on.

"Hurry up, Heaven, we don't have a lot of time." She glanced at her watch. "Shift change occurs in ten minutes, and one of the guards waits until the previous shift leaves before sneaking out for a cigarette."

"Okay," I mumbled. I put on the jeans and sweatshirt she'd handed me, then laced up the tennis shoes. I sat on the bed ready to go. Syl kept looking at her watch. I guessed that about fifteen minutes had passed when she poked her head out the door and motioned for me to follow her.

We hurried down the hall, and she used her security badge to move us through three separate checkpoints. I thought we were home free when we reached her car, until I heard a man call out, "Stop right there, Dr. Krause. I don't want to have to shoot you."

"Get in, Heaven," Syl directed, as she slid quickly into the driver's seat.

I hadn't even had a chance to shut the door or buckle myself in before she screeched off. I managed to close the door and began fumbling with the seat belt. I didn't think I would survive this car ride, but I'd rather die in the car with Syl than strapped in the chair in the midst of their regimen of torture.

Syl was probably a race car driver in her previous life. We barreled past the guard in front of the gate. Her heavy-duty SUV made mincemeat of the gate as it began to close. I suspect the startled guard realized we were making a break, but he'd been a bit too slow to close the gate.

I tried to keep the bile from surfacing, as Syl took our tail on a wild goose chase. I decided not to sneak another look when I noticed the speedometer reach 100. I guessed that Syl had given me a placebo instead of my normal meds, because I was far too alert, feeling every twist and turn in the road. At that moment, I almost wished for a trip back to zombie land.

Syl kept looking in the rearview mirror and finally lowered her speed. Her self-satisfied expression alerted me that we'd finally shaken whomever was following us.

"Can you please pull over for a second?" I croaked.

Syl looked again in her mirror, nodded, and eased onto the side of the road. I opened the door and puked before I asked, "What do we do now? You know they'll find us."

"I know some influential people. Trust me, it will all work out. I promise."

I didn't believe everything would work out and only hoped for a small amount of time when my life wouldn't be filled with pain and loss. I never in a million years would have imagined the roller coaster ride ahead.

CHAPTER ONE

I wiped away the tiny crumbs that had gathered in the corners of my eyes, otherwise known as sleep crusties. The contentment that was slowly forming a smile on my face met my best mate's stony glare. I froze mid grin.

Syl, my roommate and best friend, my only friend, had opened my bedroom door wide. She pointed to the voluptuous woman, whose eyes were darting around the room, just one second short of full-on panic. "I believe this one is attached to you. You didn't take your fucking meds again, did you?"

"Can't I please keep her for thirty minutes? That's all I need," I pleaded.

Syl shook her head. "Heaven, I did not bring her to your bedroom to satisfy one of your fantasies. It's a good thing I love you, because you are still the craziest damn woman I've ever met. What if you had…?"

She let the statement dangle in the air. Last time I'd foregone taking my meds, the hairy monster I'd conjured up barely made it back into never-never land before one of his razor-sharp claws landed on Syl's back. She wasn't very happy with me at the time. The hypodermic needle she'd jammed into my ass while dodging bigfoot was wielded like a dagger. I'd sported a big bruise for over a week, and she'd said it served me right for dancing along the edge again. I think she mumbled something like, *fucking woman never learns*.

"We can do this the easy way or the hard way," Syl said.

"One kiss?" I bargained.

Syl held up the hypodermic needle. "Hard way, rightio." She lunged for the bed and had me on my stomach in one swift move.

I yelped when the needle found its mark and sent me back into anti-dreamland.

†

When I rolled over and felt the soreness in my right cheek, I remembered the early-morning hope bubble Syl burst before it formed. I thought of an overly repulsive pimple, squeezed and bursting from the skin. I was reminded of why Syl was my only friend.

I owed Syl my current freedom and wondered why I felt compelled to test her loyalty and patience toward me. She was a government scientist who'd grown a conscience. I'd long since forgiven her for her earlier participation in the secret dream program. We both knew, deep inside, that my freedom was only temporary. It hadn't exactly been easy to escape from Spartan and Turnbull, but with their resources, they should have easily apprehended us before we managed to leave the compound. Things weren't adding up. Two plus two did not equal four.

There was no limit to the demented ways our government found to put itself at the top of the heap. Superpower with the Most Egregious Weapons was the name of the game. Psychopaths. The whole lot of them were an elite and very intelligent group of crazies, who thought up creative ways to topple the other emerging superpowers. I got the feeling they would be stepping up their game, now that a maniac was in office who condoned enhanced interrogation and other military tactics. It was 2017, and in many ways, we'd taken a huge step backward that demonstrated the lengths we would go to regarding individual freedoms for our own citizens. Exploiting teens was an acceptable casualty in the war against terror.

I rubbed my sore ass and toppled out of bed. Taking my index finger to the corners of my eyes, I wiped away the crusties. Like the crumbs from my favorite chocolate chip cookies, they scattered across my small chest and landed on my tank top. Two little grapes, that's about all I had, not even a handful. I might as well have been a guy for how much God had decided to bestow on me. At least, I was blessed with a decent face and good hair.

Opening the door, I peeked my head out and found Syl's cool gaze, as she sat at our kitchen table drinking her chai tea. I could smell the sweet fragrance and took it as a good sign. Maybe she wouldn't be too pissed if she was relaxing with a cup of chai. I swiveled my head from right to left, looking for the woman.

Syl arched her eyebrow. "Really, Heaven?"

"There's always a first time. Remember the motto, whatever you can think up…"

"And that's why we came up with an antidote. Shutting down your creations is a full-time job." Syl took a sip of her tea and sighed. "Sit down, Heaven. We need to have a heart to heart. I can't keep doing this."

I shuffled into the room and sat heavily on the zebra-wood chair. It was beautiful wood but not very kind on my already sore behind. "It was just one night, and I was having a really good day. I knew I'd only conjure up something nice…well, nice for me. You already have someone." I started to pour myself a cup of tea.

"That's what I wanted to talk to you about. Listen, the only reason that I haven't moved in with Darla yet is…"

My head popped up, and I felt the heat rise to my face. My good mood was taking a turn in the wrong direction. "So, I'm some kind of charity case? Is that what you've been doing? Gotta make sure the Dream Weaver doesn't create havoc. We can't have that now, can we? Too bad your pals didn't consider the consequences of turning a crazy, bipolar woman into a Weaver. Oh wait, that's exactly what you hoped to develop. That dark side does make the best weapons, now doesn't it? Why didn't you guys just pick on the normal, run-of-the-mill sociopaths, you know, your brothers and sisters in crime?" I was on a roll. I took a deep breath and was about to continue my rant, when Syl held up her hand. She pinched her nose and appeared to gather her energy.

I didn't want to take a journey down memory lane, the road wasn't easy to travel, but the conversation sparked the memory, and I was forced to remember our time in the Dream Center.

Spartan had me strapped to the chair again. Steel plates kept my head in place, so I couldn't look away. It was an ingenious method of keeping my eyes forward to take in every ghastly scene on the state-of-the-art, seventy-inch, flat-screen TV. Only the best for Spartan's house of torture.

I wanted to close my eyes, but Dr. Spartan wouldn't let me. If I blocked out the horror for more than five seconds, the increased current would send a shock of pain into my body. Eventually, I couldn't resist anymore. I would relent when the pain grew too great.

I never knew where they dug up the various horror flicks, war movies, or other sick psychological thrillers. I knew they weren't mainstream. I wouldn't put it past the Dream Center to hire their own movie crew and create the most gruesome visual displays some psychopath's warped brain could dream up. It was their idea for a primer to send me to the dark place, so I could conjure up something equally horrific.

On a particularly arduous session, I knew I might not survive the electric current that increased each time I slammed my eyelids and shut out the images. Death was the lesser of two evils. I always got the sense that he enjoyed delivering pain to me. Syl saved my life that day, when she walked into Spartan's favorite room.

"Are you out of your fucking mind?" the woman's voice asked.

I felt the electrodes being ripped from my body. I carefully opened my eyes and said a prayer when I saw Syl standing in front of the TV, blocking the dreadful images. I hadn't recognized her voice; I tried to shield myself from everything in that room, to keep the images from burning into my subconscious mind.

I could almost taste the shock and regret that emanated from her eyes. It wasn't exactly pity I saw, but I knew the sight before her was dire. I must have looked like dog crap.

"How dare you interfere in my training session? Go back to your lab Dr. Krause and finish refining that serum we need," Spartan said through gritted teeth.

With an eerie calm, Syl responded, "If you kill Heaven, she won't help you achieve your goals. I believe that Mr. Turnbull has special plans for her, and I wouldn't want to be in your shoes if this asset is lost due to your incompetence. I think it would be prudent to have him see for himself how your methods impact our precious resource." After she spun on her heel and left the room, Spartan called in one of his lackeys to supervise.

I understood why when Turnbull burst through the door. "You moron. Get her to the infirmary. If she expires, I'll have your head."

"Yes, sir."

After the debacle with the dead scientist and my out-of-control apparitions, Syl was assigned to control me. I didn't have a clue why the government thought it was a good idea to experiment with someone who was bipolar, but it seemed like the most successful Dream Weavers were those with personality disorders. It was ironic how the scientists could control the worst sociopaths, but they weren't able to control me. Six researchers had lost their lives in the pursuit of science. That actuality just made me more unpredictable, as I blamed myself for every single loss of life resulting from my creations. I did discover, later, that an apparition that wasn't even mine had caused the biggest loss in my life.

Nevertheless, it was a never-ending spiral. Something bad would happen, and I would go darker.

Syl had always been kind whenever she had to inject me with a new drug. I knew she was taking extra care to hurt me as little as possible. I saw the compassion in her eyes, and I was grateful for the reprieve from my training sessions. Syl hadn't been around lately, because they were starting a new regime and controlling me was no longer their objective. I think they believed they were on the verge of a breakthrough that would allow me to create and control my monsters.

Two weeks later, when I had sufficiently recovered from Dr. Spartan's overambitious training, Syl found a way to take me away from the Dream Center. I didn't have a better alternative, and deep down, I did trust Syl.

I had put my life in her hands back then, and I was still in her care. I shook myself back to the present and our conversation.

"I have a solution. Darla knows this Dream Catcher—"

The wood chair scraped across the floor as I abruptly stood. "Forget it. I'm not going." I crossed my arms over my chest.

Syl sighed again. "God, you are impossible. She's a lesbian, and she's just your type. Curvy in all the right places. Darla says she's a real sweetheart. She's offered to work with you for free."

My eyes narrowed. I was skeptical. "Why? What's in it for her?"

"Darla told her about you, and she wants to meet you. She's only met the low-level Weavers and is intrigued by your abilities."

I leaned against the wall. "Catchers are worse than shrinks. The meds are bad enough, and now you want to sic their fancy mojo on me."

"One time…it was one time. How was I to know the Catcher was sent by—"

"Spartan," I finished for her. "Now there's a real sweetheart. Why didn't he volunteer one of his star lab rats? I can't imagine he would dream up anything less for the total annihilation of our…" I made the symbol for quotation marks "…enemies."

"You know the answer to that," she answered.

I did know the answer to that. We both knew they were just biding their time. Neither one of us was a fool; we knew they'd allowed us to get away. I was too valuable to them, and they knew Syl was the only person who could control me. Talent like mine was rare, very rare. There were a handful of us that could do what we did, but like any maniacal experiment, there were always unanticipated side effects. The side effects were the final straw for Syl. Finally, she recognized the dangerous game they were playing.

We knew there was an underground group, but no one knew how some of the Catchers managed to escape and stay free. They remained on the fringe, just outside of Turnbull's control. There were even rumors that a few low-level Weavers were free. That gave me hope.

"We've both made mistakes, but I trust Darla. She has a sixth sense about people. In her own way, she's as talented as you are. Will you please just meet the Catcher? And for God's sake, take your damn meds in the meantime. I don't know how it all works, or how long it takes for a Catcher to settle a Weaver."

I felt defeated. I knew I was a drain on Syl's energy. She needed a break from me. Even when I took my meds, a dream could slip through. She'd laid her own life on the line to put several of my genies back in the bottle.

I started laughing when I remembered the sex-crazed pole dancer I'd summoned, who ignored me and zeroed in on Syl. It was the first time I'd lied to her. I swore I'd taken the meds. She wasn't prepared for her. I had to listen to her lecture about reckless behavior for over a week.

Darla was beyond pissed when the dancer began rubbing her body against Syl, but she got over it. I liked Darla. She had a sense of confidence that always made me feel settled.

"Sometimes my talent is fun…" I doubled over laughing.

"This is not funny, Heaven. You're playing with fire, and all of us are going to receive third degree burns by mere association." She growled to emphasize her point.

"Okay, I'll meet the damn Dream Sucker."

"Catcher. Don't you even think about throwing derogatory comments her way. You know how much they hate being called that," Syl warned.

"Catcher, sucker, same dif." I rolled my eyes.

"Fine Ms. Dream Screamer."

"Mean. You're just plain mean. All right, point taken. I'll be nice. She better be as hot as you say. Do you think she'd have sex with me?"

"Heaven!"

"All right, all right. I was just kidding."

I wasn't kidding. I hadn't been intimate with anyone in over two years. Who wanted to take the chance that a huge scaly monster would nestle between the sheets in the middle of the night after hours of mind-blowing sex? Or that a voluptuous woman would barge in on an intimate moment for a ménage a trois I'd imagined. More than one woman left me in a huff over that stunt.-Not that I was skilled enough to give my partner phenomenal sex. Any intimacy that ended my drought would blow my mind. It was hard to keep the fact that I was a Dream Weaver under wraps after the first few disastrous liaisons.

"So, when is this little blind date set up for?"

"It is not a blind date. She's coming over for dinner."

"Fine, you're cooking." That was an unnecessary declaration. We both knew that. I couldn't even manage to boil water without burning the pan.

CHAPTER TWO

I stood in front of my closet, contemplating my choices. I didn't have a whole lot to choose from. Syl got me a job as a phlebotomist at the hospital she'd returned to after leaving The Dream Team. It didn't pay a lot.

The health system had combined behavioral and physical health a few years back. The government mandate made sense at the time. Mental health patients kept showing up in their emergency department, and until they built the mental health wing, there was no place to put them.

Before the government got their nasty mitts into me, I'd ended up in an ED that wasn't adequately equipped to deal with kids like me. My parents were even less prepared to handle my quirks. I suppose I was lucky that the pills I took weren't enough to do me in like I'd planned. Once they got me settled, the hospital wasn't able to hold me beyond the two-day evaluation period. Off I went, hoping for my next high. I was extremely productive when I was on a high. I could go days without sleep and any type of work was a breeze for me.

Work. Right. All my shirts were lined up in a neat row from dark to light. I pulled out the red one; I wanted her to notice me. Screw Syl. If the woman really was just my type, I was going to consider this a date.

I moved to the end of the closet and picked out a pair of black jeans. They were tight enough to show that I still attended to my body, regardless of my mental problems, but loose enough not to scream slut.

After buttoning up my shirt and wiggling into my jeans, I looked in the floor-to-ceiling mirror. I tried to assess what the Dream Catcher would see. I looked okay, I guess. Maybe she wouldn't notice the big bags under my eyes. I wasn't stupid. When I stopped taking my meds, I knew what could occur. Sleep wasn't a high priority until I knew my mood was on the lighter side. Unfortunately, that only improved recently. I'd gone several days without sleep and without Syl finding out.

Syl had figured out that the same meds used to control my bipolar disorder, with a few minor modifications, controlled my dreams. No dreams, no monsters. No dreams, no joy either. The meds leveled me out so much, I might as well have been a zombie. *Why don't people understand that's no way to live? I don't feel a thing when I regularly take my meds. Not hate and certainly not love. I want to feel love.*

I smiled in the mirror. The shot in the ass might have removed my dream woman, but it hadn't provided the full effect of my normal meds. I was still in a good mood, and when I was like this, I could charm the pants off a devout, straight Christian. Of course, part of my disorder was a distorted sense of reality. Whether I was really that charming, or not, was up for debate. I left my most prominent feature hanging loose, my long blonde hair.

I nearly skipped into the kitchen.

†

Syl was stirring a large pot. I peered over her shoulder and sniffed. Her very tasty spaghetti sauce was bubbling away. The aromatic garlic and herbs made my mouth water.

"Hiya roomy. Mmmm that smells delicious. What time are Darla and her friend coming over?" I smiled wide.

Syl narrowed her eyes. "Do you know how tempted I am to crush your meds into your dinner? But I can never count on you to be consistent. It would be just my luck that you'd take them before we eat, just to spite me, and then OD in front of Darla."

I danced around the kitchen. "Aw don't be like that." I grabbed her hand and twirled her around. "Let's put on 'Macarena' and dance."

The doorbell interrupted us, and I ran to answer it. Distorted perception be damned, Darla's friend was exquisite. She *was* curvy in all the right places. I wasn't attracted to half-starved models. I liked women with enough soft spots to sink my teeth into. She had thick, chestnut hair that settled on her shoulders; and I could definitely get lost in those emerald-green eyes that were large, but not too large for her face. When she smiled, her even, white teeth sat between two deep dimples. I was a sucker for dimples. She had an almost exotic look about her, and I was smitten.

"Hiya, Darla." I grabbed her and squeezed. I wanted to show the gorgeous woman that I was a friendly, affectionate sort, not afraid to wrap up those close to me in a warm and fuzzy hug. I finally let Syl's girlfriend go and looked expectantly in her direction, waiting for her to make the introductions.

Darla smiled at me. "You must be having a good day."

"I am, and I must say I am dying, well not literally, to meet this goddess standing in front of me." I stuck out my hand.

A slow, sexy smile spread across the face of my desire, as she extended her own hand and uttered one word, "Maya."

I took her hand and offered her a feather like kiss. I knew this was old-school cheesiness, but her smile remained. "It is my absolute pleasure to meet you. I'm Heavenlaya, but my close friends call me Heaven."

"Hmmm, Heavenlaya, that's an unusual name," Maya said.

I motioned for them to come in. "My mom and dad couldn't settle on one name, so they combined them. Syl's been slaving over a hot stove. I have many talents, but cooking is not one of them. I hope you won't hold that against me. I guess you'll have to be the chef in our family when we get married."

"Sorry, I won't agree to marry anyone I haven't test driven." Maya sashayed into the room.

"You know, I just took a shower, so I have that new car smell. You can take a test drive anytime you want." I was shamelessly flirting now.

"I'll definitely have to consider that option. New car smell, that's funny." Maya chuckled.

I gestured that my heart was pounding out of my chest and grinned. I danced next to Syl and whispered in her ear, "It's kinda shaping up to be a date after all."

She shook her head, but I saw the small smile on her face. Syl was all bark and no bite.

†

I decided to ease off on the charm while we ate, mainly because I was starving and I couldn't focus on making Maya swoon at the same time I was stuffing a sopped piece of garlic bread in my mouth. One relatively manageable side effect of the experimental drugs I took, or those shoved into me, was a ravenous appetite.

When Syl pulled out the wine and only poured a glass for Maya, Darla, and herself, Maya raised her eyebrow but didn't say a word. Syl was trying to be surreptitious, but not a whole lot escaped Maya's keen observation. The shot that Syl jabbed into my bum earlier that day did not mix well with alcohol. The drug wasn't exactly approved by the Food and Drug Administration, but Syl knew all of the contraindications for its use. She'd certainly used it on me enough to know what to avoid and what was safe.

I'd just shoved a large forkful of spaghetti into my mouth, when Maya offhandedly asked, "You're bipolar, right?"

I thought all the heavy talk would wait until after dinner, but she'd asked the question in the same manner she might solicit me to pass her the salt.

The mouthful of red sauce and slimy noodles I spewed all over Syl's beautiful table wasn't a pretty sight. "What?" I sputtered.

"Bipolar," she said. "Most of the especially talented Dream Weavers the government goes after are bipolar to the extreme. I just figured that's why you need my help." She took a bite of bread.

"Um…"

"Oh, do you prefer I call it something else—maybe go with the old-school terminology—manic-depressive?" Maya asked. "Personally, I think that sounds, well, depressing. I think they should rename it something completely neutral, like Gemini Syndrome. Or perhaps, just Gemini, because disorders and syndromes seem to suggest that something is terribly wrong with the person. I think you have a rare and wonderful gift."

Syl was looking at Maya like she had two heads or something. I could almost hear Syl's thoughts. *Don't encourage her. It's already a pain in the ass to get her to take her meds.*

My mouth hung open for a second before I thought to close it, knowing it wasn't a very attractive look for me. "You're not afraid of my dark moods? You think dream weaving is a gift?"

She nodded. "Of course I do. The gift just needs a tiny bit of direction." Maya lifted her hand, her thumb and index finger showing her idea of tiny.

Darla was beaming next to Maya. "I told you she was brilliant."

Syl's expression was sour. I couldn't figure out if it was because this woman was encouraging me to bypass my meds—at least that was my interpretation—or because Darla seemed as enamored with Maya as I clearly was. Of course, Syl could be using reverse psychology on me. I had a hard time separating fact from fiction. Was Syl play acting so I would jump on the chance to work with this alluring Dream Catcher? I didn't really care, because I'd already swallowed the hook.

"So....what would it entail, if I agreed to work with you?" I might have been a little tentative in the way I asked the question. After all, I wasn't going to just lay open my brain for her to poke around in without limits.

Maya showed me her pearly whites, and I got the distinct impression that she knew she'd almost reeled me in. I hadn't put up a big fight, maybe not any resistance at all. She had glorious bosoms, perfect chestnut-colored hair, and dimples. What would you expect?

I kept looking between her perfect smile, and the creamy tops of her breasts that didn't even pretend to remain locked away within her bra. They were practically standing on their tippy toes, waving hello to me. I wondered, briefly, if she wore a push-up bra. Did she wear that especially for me? Did it really matter?

"It could take several months of intensive one-on-one work. Are you willing to work hard with me, just the two of us?"

I nodded. I felt like I was in a trance. She'd hypnotized me with her gorgeous, green eyes and her smile and those lovely ta tas.

"Good. We'll start tomorrow."

And that was where my journey began. Unfortunately, outside forces weren't going to make things easy on any of us.

CHAPTER THREE

I could tell that Syl really wanted to follow Darla to her place and have wild, tear your clothes off, feel it the next day, sex, but she knew she had to babysit me. I could turn on a dime. I'd done it before; the nasty scar on Syl's shoulder was a daily reminder of that.

Syl closed the front door, and we walked back into the living room. She had a glass of wine in her hand. I had flat sparkling water.

"Maybe this wasn't such a great idea," Syl began.

I put my water on the coffee table, then plopped my ass on the love seat. "Oh, no you don't. I like her. I think she can help me, us. You're the one that suggested this."

"She's not what I expected." Syl sat in the recliner. Her mouth did that worried thing as one half of her lip scrunched to the other side.

"Yeah well, me either. She was refreshingly direct and so beautiful." I'm sure my dreamy expression caused Syl more concern. "Did you see how her breast peeked deliciously out from her shirt? One more button, and I'll bet I could have seen her bra—probably some sexy Victoria's Secret, lace creation. Mmmm, yeah, one more button."

"You know, I'm beginning to re-evaluate a few things. I should just take you to a professional, so you can get it all out of your system. Maybe then you would be able to think more clearly. I suppose not having sex for so long has clouded your judgment..."

"Syl, you know that my...uh...special gift twists my sense of reality with unique perceptions. A romp in the sack with an escort isn't going to alter that, but I do have my very lucid moments. I really think this is one of them. I get a good feeling about Maya. I believe she can help me."

"Assist you in what way, that's the real question. If it's to help scratch a long overdue itch, that's not solving the problem." Syl brought the glass of wine to her lips and took a sip.

"Maybe you're the one too focused on sex, because you didn't get to go home with Darla and *your* perception is off. I meant, she could relieve me of my nasty dream apparitions, not assist me with my long, dry spell of unwanted abstinence."

"We'll see. I have a bad feeling about what is on the horizon for all of us."

"Maybe it's just indigestion from your spaghetti sauce. There was an awful lot of garlic in it," I quipped.

Sylt threw a pillow at me. "I'd like to see you do better. Oh wait, you don't cook. I have several charred pots to prove it."

"I could learn. Do you think that would impress Maya?"

"You have bigger issues to tackle. I probably wouldn't worry about your ineptness in the kitchen. Please, don't go falling in love or lust. It only serves to exacerbate your condition. Need I remind you what happened when Twyla broke up with you after you'd only been dating for one week?"

"It isn't fair that you get to plan for a future with Darla, but all I can hope for is periodic visits to a *professional*." I knew I was pouting, but she wasn't being reasonable.

"Life isn't fair, Heaven. I'm sorry you got dealt a bad hand." She looked at me with pity in her eyes, and I thought she really was sorry.

"Is my disorder so bad that I don't deserve love?" I wanted to know the answer.

"It's not that simple, Heaven, and you know it. When Spartan injected you with that serum to enhance your dreams, he made a typical relationship virtually impossible for you. You know that better than anyone else. I really am sorry, Heaven, for any part I played in their abominable research. I'd do anything to take it back." Syl leaned forward and pushed at her temples with her fingertips for a few seconds, almost as if she was trying to massage the bad memories away. "Maybe she can help you enough to lead a relatively normal life, but you can't get involved with a Dream Catcher. That would play right into their hands, and they might double their efforts to capture both of you."

I nodded, pretending I was in agreement with her, but in my mind, I was crossing my fingers behind my back. A painful memory entered my mind. Rosie was a Catcher, and we were a good team. "Of course you're right, Syl, you always are." I tried to keep the edge out of my voice. I wasn't sure I'd succeeded when I saw Syl's eyes narrow and bore into me, attempting to seek the truth.

It probably seemed like the only thing I had on my mind was sex, but what I really craved was love. I wanted someone to look at me with adoration in their eyes, the way that Syl looked at Darla. I was tired of people either treating me like a leper, or manipulating me so they could release my "true potential." It had been a long time since I'd seen that look of absolute adulation. Ever since the tragedy, every single woman I'd managed to start a relationship wanted something from me. Maya was the first person to offer her services with no strings attached, and she thought of my disorder as a gift. In my mind, that was a double plus. As far as I could tell, she didn't operate under the rules of WIIFM. So far, she hadn't asked, "What's in it for me?"

Was I in love? Of course not, but I was in serious like.

Having Syl as my only friend wasn't enough for me anymore; and now that she was about to abandon me, I'd have nothing, no one in my life. If that wasn't enough to conjure up my dark side, I didn't know what else would do the trick. If only those government hacks knew that isolation was such an effective tool. They'd be salivating.

I looked closely at Syl. Maybe that was the plan all along. Perhaps she was there to gain my trust, then—bam—pull the rug out from under me and slide me into a dark tunnel. I shook my head. Paranoid thoughts began to creep inside.

"What's going on in your un-medicated little brain?" Syl asked.

I showed her my teeth. "Nothing."

"I've known you long enough to recognize that look. Can't you please take at least a half dose of your meds? I promise, if this Catcher can help, you can wean yourself off of the meds completely. We'll find a way to manage the small peaks and valleys. You know we can't keep pulling you from the clouds or the depths of hell. Your moods swings aren't manageable anymore, after your stint in the special research wing. Going from Mount Everest to Jules Verne's bloody center of the earth is becoming increasingly unpredictable. I care about you, Heaven, and really just want what's best for you."

"Do you, Syl? Do you really, or are you about ready to hand me over again? They'll probably give you a healthy chunk of change, and you'll get your happily ever after with Darla. You never told me your middle name, but Syl Judas Bell does have a nice ring to it." I started laughing. "Get it, bell, ring?"

"Don't make me pull out the hypodermic. You know how I hate doing that to you. I only reserve it for desperate moments when some hairy beast is about to bite my head off. Think about it, Heaven. Why would I go to the trouble of pulling your ass out of the fire, just to toss you back in?"

I shrugged. "You getting me out was just too damn easy. I'm not hallucinating that black vehicle parked two blocks from our house, or the other one that follows me to work."

Syl bit her lip. "No, you're not hallucinating. I saw them," Syl admitted.

"Why can't they just leave me alone?" I cried out, as I put my head in my hands and began sobbing. I was moving into hell now, and that was a very bad thing. The severity of my illness caused radical shifts in mere minutes. Anything could set off the chain reaction.

Syl jumped up off the couch and squatted in front of me. "Heaven, look at me."

I looked into her eyes and saw only compassion. I had to believe she really did care, because no one else was in my corner.

"I'm not the enemy. You are such a beautiful person, inside and out, but I worry. Please, let me get your pills. You can start tomorrow with Maya, like she suggested. I'll take you to her place myself and make sure she does right by you. I promise, everything is going to work out."

Damn, my memories would not leave me alone. I just had to revisit the day we escaped. At the time, it seemed like I'd finally be free of the Dream Center, once and for all. I placed all my hope in Syl. I figured Syl had to be smarter than a couple of kids learning to live on their own. We thought they'd leave us alone, because we weren't worth the hassle.

I nodded once. I would take the damn drugs, because if I hit bottom, there was no telling what kind of monster I would conjure up. They were usually hairy. I'm not sure why.

I watched her shuffle into the other room through my bleary eyes. When she came back with two blue pills and picked up the glass of water, she handed them to me without saying a word. I took them like an obedient child. Maya would soon come face to face with the nondescript zombie, a pale version of who I really am. My flat affect might scare her worse than my depressive state, but Syl was right, we couldn't take a chance. The only other time I'd been able to control my monsters was when I was with Rosie. I wasn't about to let my traitorous brain go back in time again to the only happy memories I had of the Dream Center, so I pushed Rosie from my mind, again.

CHAPTER FOUR

The quiet knock on the door wasn't what stirred me from sleep. No, that was Satan, my all-black cat. When I failed to pet him after he lightly put his paw on my chest, he bit my chin.

"What the fuck, Satan? No bites." I pushed his face away and flicked him on the nose. He was still learning that biting his mom was not exactly going to achieve the desired results. He changed his tactic and licked my face, so I acquiesced and started moving my hand through his long fur.

I laid in bed for at least an hour, doing nothing, really. I wasn't sad, just unmotivated. The knock on the door was neither welcome nor dreaded. After a double dose of meds, I felt very little. I'm not even sure I'd traveled up the feeling thermometer to apathy. Nothingness. It's what I loathed about the medication. Of course, I didn't have *that* particular emotion on the morning I was to begin my work with Maya. Hate was definitely something that I only felt while off my meds.

I ignored the knock. It took too much energy to say come in, and I knew Syl would enter anyway. She opened the door a crack and slipped inside my bedroom. "I made your favorite breakfast." She looked sheepish. "You still have about an hour before you have to head over to Maya's. Do you want me to come with or at least drive you over?"

"No." A one-word answer was all I could muster.

"How do you feel this morning?"

"Flat."

"Are you up for this? Do you want me to call and rearrange for a session later this week?"

I shrugged. "No."

Syl paused before nodding and closing the door.

I shuffled into the bathroom and slowly performed my morning ritual. Habits were easy to manage, emotions not so much. I didn't want to bother with my thick mop, so I grabbed a hair tie and pulled my blonde locks into a messy ponytail. I squinted in the mirror, appraising my hair. I don't know why my hair never turned dark as I got older; it stayed an almost golden color. It helped getting those first dates. Too bad nice hair wasn't enough to keep women interested after they found out about my living, breathing, dreams.

Syl must have felt guilty, because when I sat down at the kitchen table, she blurted, "I'm sorry, Heaven. I know you hate how the medication takes away your joy, but you were heading in the opposite direction last night and..." She poured hot water into my apple spice tea.

"It's okay, Syl. I get it."

Syl jabbed her fork into the French toast on the table and added three pieces to my plate. Her sigh could have been heard around the world, as she sat heavily in the chair across from me. "God, I hate seeing you like this. Maya better be the miracle worker Darla swears she is, or I'm going to start popping those blue pills. Right now, I feel like a total shit."

I cut into a piece of toast and started chewing. I didn't think she expected an answer, and I didn't care enough to try to form words that would make her feel better. I'd already mentioned it was okay, so I wasn't sure what else she wanted me to say. We finished breakfast in relative silence. She appeared uncomfortable. I didn't care one way or the other.

In the center of the table lay the directions to Maya's house that she'd written so carefully. After loading the dishwasher, I picked up the sheet of paper and studied the directions. They seemed straightforward enough.

I grabbed my jacket and headed for the door. "See you later." Habit kicked in and allowed me to say the appropriate thing before heading to Maya's.

"If you need me to come, just call," I heard Syl say before I gently closed the door.

†

I climbed into my old beater and rolled by the black SUV that was a perpetual accessory in our neighborhood. It didn't piss me off this morning, when the car followed me all the way to Maya's. I suppose that was a good thing.

My feet dragged along on the pavement, as I made my way to her door. I pushed the lighted bear, dog, or some kind of animal paw print and rang the bell. When Maya answered

29

the door and squeezed me tight with an overambitious hug, the first smile of the day made its way to my face.

After she let me go, her head tilted to the side and her eyes narrowed. "You took your medication last night, didn't you?"

I nodded. "It was necessary."

She looked over my shoulder, and I turned my head to see what she was intently focused on. The black vehicle rolled slowly by. I shrugged.

"I don't suppose they try to hide their interest in your every move, but I don't much like having those assholes scrutinize *my* actions." Maya turned to her side and waved me in. "Take a seat on the couch, I'll be right back."

She darted out the door, and I briefly wondered what she was about to do. I didn't care enough to trail her, so I followed her directive, like a good soldier, and took a seat on her couch.

I stared at her soothing, sage-colored wall and sat patiently awaiting my host, with my hands clasped together in my lap. I couldn't tell you whether it was ten minutes or ten hours; time was fuzzy at best.

Without real interest, I turned my head when Maya came barreling into the room, huffing and puffing. Even in my flat state, I could tell she was pissed.

"This will not do. No, this will never do," she mumbled and those emerald eyes flashed. "I simply cannot work with those medieval constraints to my psychic energy."

"Just ignore them. It's what I do, and for the most part, it works."

"The douchebag had the nerve to smirk at me. I don't tolerate smirkers. He's about to dream about having the runs all night long, which will trigger loose bowels and make it his reality for the next two days." Maya smirked.

I thought it was ironic that she smirked but didn't tolerate that in others. I almost said something, but she waved her hand in the air. "I get to smirk, because I'm one of the good guys."

Every minute that passed allowed me to become more engaged in my surroundings and interactions with others. "How'd you know that was what I was thinking?"

"Heaven, you're not the only one they experimented on. I have special skills they can't even fathom. I'm going to help you, Heaven, because I can and because I want to stick it to them every chance I get. But they can never know how much power I have. They have no idea, what talents they unleashed in either one of us. No matter what, you can't ever tell them."

"I have no fucking idea what you're talking about, other than knowing what they did to me, so no worries there."

Maya seemed to appraise me, and I squirmed under her scrutiny. When she nodded her head and went to her kitchen without a word, I guessed that I had passed muster. I heard her clanging around and wiggled my butt as I settled into the cushy sofa. I brushed my hand along the soft fabric. Ultrasuede was my favorite, because it was soft to the touch. I actually preferred the synthetic microfiber over leather.

I was still trying to shake the effects of the drugs, as they slowly began to dissipate. Exercise would have helped me to metabolize them more quickly and ultimately move the chemicals out, but I rarely wanted to do anything after taking a double dose.

I don't recall what I was thinking when Maya returned with a glass of wine in one hand and a tall glass of amber liquid. The condensation on the outside dripped along the sides, and I watched intently as the droplets made their way to the bottom.

"Sorry, wine for me but iced tea for you. Maybe the caffeine will hurry along your recovery from those damn chemicals. I can't help you if you continue to take that poison."

I arched my eyebrow. "You actually want me to stop taking my meds?"

Maya blessed me with her beautiful smile. "Of course. I thought you understood that. I'm going to teach you how to control and redirect your gift. When you're in the driver's seat at all times, they can't manipulate you. The chemicals stunt your abilities and that just will not do." She tsked as she set the glass on the table.

"Syl will never agree to that," I stated flatly. "She has legitimate reasons…and it is rather selfish of me to continue to place her at risk."

"Oh, you let me worry about Syl. Besides you'll be staying here with me. We need to talk about how to make that happen."

With that little bombshell, she spun around and headed back to the kitchen, returning shortly with two plates of steaming pasta. She set them on the solid oak dining table and motioned for me to come sit.

I grabbed my iced tea, looking longingly at her glass of wine. I breathed in the almost sweet aroma from the creamy heap of lobster mac and cheese. It smelled heavenly, and I marveled at my ability to appreciate the offering. Sometimes the meds would blunt my olfactory glands, but that never stopped me from feeling rapacious.

"Dig in," Maya directed, as she joined me at the table. I waited while she took a sip of her wine. The blush of the wine matched the color of her lips. I watched intently, suddenly ravenous for a completely different reason. I wondered about the wine choice. I always thought that white wine went best with seafood, but it seemed like Maya didn't adhere to any strict rules on pairing.

She grinned at me, and I just knew she could decipher what I was thinking. When she grabbed her fork and scooped up her first bite, I followed and dug in with gusto.

"Oh, my God, this is delicious. You are a goddess. Will you marry me? Because I don't think I've ever had a better pasta. Now, I know I'm definitely in love," I joked.

She ignored my comments and launched into her own agenda. "Heaven, we'll need to do some intensive work over the next several months. You'll move in with me and share the household chores, except for cooking. I get the impression you don't do much of that. I don't require any compensation other than, after you've finished, I want you to help me with the others."

"The others?" I felt my brow furrow. I wasn't sure who she was talking about.

"Yes, the other women they've experimented on. The ones like us. Most of them aren't as powerful as you or me, so they won't be as difficult. We can't let those dicknobs win. You know that, don't you?"

"Do you mean the government?"

"Yes of course. The government can't win; they won't use the power wisely. They never have, and they never will. We're expendable pawns in their little wars." She caught my eyes and held them.

"They'll never let me go. They're just allowing me to take a minivacation. I'm smart enough to know that's why they keep tabs on me. Syl tries to ignore the surveillance, but she knows it too. It only took them a week to find us."

"Oh, Heaven, you have no idea how much power you have, but you'll learn. You do know the difference between Catchers and Weavers, right?"

I shrugged. I had the basic concepts but not the nitty gritty details. That didn't stop me from answering with confidence as I gave her the broad strokes. "Weavers bring to life the creations in their dreams, and Catchers somehow control them."

"You have a big hole in your knowledge base." She steered the conversation in another direction and made it clear the plans were settled.

I wasn't sure whether I was exchanging one prison for another. Time would tell. At least this prison had a very sexy guard to look at.

CHAPTER FIVE

"What? Are you out of your fucking mind?" Syl screamed through the phone. I'd called to say I was planning to stay the night and that I'd be by the following day to collect some things I would need while I lived at Maya's for the next three months. I asked her to take care of Satan while I was gone. She grumbled, but I knew she would never let my baby starve.

Maya gestured for me to hand her the phone. "Hello Syl," she said in that silky-smooth voice of hers. "You have to trust me. I know what I'm doing... Yes, I know the risks... No, we won't need her medication... Syl, you need to calm down. You're going to cause yourself an aneurism."

I left the room at that point. It seemed like Maya was able to handle Syl far better than me, and I didn't want to listen when they started talking about me like I was a piece of furniture. I knew they would, eventually.

Maya had a lovely back deck. The sun was beginning to set with a painter's long, broad strokes of red, yellow, and orange bleeding into the bright, blue backdrop.

A part of me was nervous about staying with Maya, but another piece of me was screaming yes! I knew it was too much to hope for, as I started to fantasize about playing house with this beautiful woman. I began to wonder where I might sleep. Maybe she'd have to watch me so closely that I would get to sleep with her, a hair's breath away from an errant hand brushing over her creamy skin in the middle of the night. One thing would lead to another and I'd get to have sex again.

I probably should have been more reluctant to trust her, but she was so tempting and for whatever reason I felt an invisible connection. I hadn't experienced that in a very long time. Just because a person couldn't see or touch something, didn't mean it did not exist. That synergism was there, just beneath the surface, waiting to explode.

The sliding-glass door made a subtle noise as it opened, and suddenly Maya was standing in front of me smiling broadly. "It's all set. I'll give you some sleepwear and get you settled in the guest bedroom."

Damn. That was not what I was wishing for. I forced the corners of my lips to turn up in what I hoped was close to a smile or at a minimum an acknowledgment that this was acceptable to me.

"Okay," I squeaked out.

"You're far too tempting to allow you into my bed just yet," she answered. "We need to give you some basic tools before we head down that path."

Now the happy dance was alighting inside my belly. I almost wanted to stick my finger in my ear and clean it out. She had just said *yet*. I was hopeful.

"Aren't you afraid I'll conjure up something big and smelly and mean?"

"We're going to do a simple meditation exercise. It isn't fail-safe, but it'll do until we get into the real training," she answered.

"I don't have a toothbrush with me." I knew that was an inane statement to make, but it was the only remotely appropriate thing that popped into my head.

Maya chuckled. "I have extras."

Extras? Just how many women did Maya invite to stay the night? We were starting to move into dangerous territory. My little green monster would ensure something very nasty would visit us tonight, as soon as I entered REM sleep.

"I collect them when I see the hygienist every six months. I don't need them with my electric toothbrush. I could toss them out, but it seems so wasteful. Good thing, huh? Now I have something to offer you."

I couldn't leave it at that. I had to go there. "Do you have a lot of women stay?"

"Nope, never. You're the first," Maya answered.

"What about the others you've helped?" I asked.

"None of them were anywhere near as special as you." She touched my arm and the goosebumps traveled all the way to the top of my head. It was a glorious tingle. I wanted to grab her and kiss her, but I was afraid I'd blow my chances, so I didn't. A small amount of the medication remained in my system and tamped down my more impulsive tendencies.

†

After I'd brushed my teeth, I went into the room that Maya showed me. It was a nice room, with calming sage accents on the bedspread. The artwork blended well with the bedding and the earth-toned walls. I felt at peace. If I didn't know any better, I would have thought the room was specially designed for people like me—someone in dire need of a calming influence in their life.

Maya casually strolled into the room after I'd turned down the bed and burrowed under the covers. She instructed me to sit up and proceeded to tuck three fluffy pillows behind my back. I wondered what we were going to do and let a tiny bit of worry creep into my body. I think she could see me tense up.

"No wonder you need meds; your violin strings are wound too tight—they're ready to break at any moment. Can you take a deep breath for me?"

She touched my diaphragm as I began to breathe in and out.

"That's great, Heaven, you're doing wonderful. Is there any place that brings back fond memories?"

I considered Maya's question and hesitated before a picture of my grandparents' home popped into my head. They'd lived out in the country, before selling the place and buying an RV to travel around. I used to marvel at how tame the deer were and how close they came to the house. Granny would lament over the deer knowing exactly when the fruit was ready. Even though they had a large orchard, my grandparents would wake up one day and find every last pear and apple stripped from the branches.

I saw the mountains and bright-green lawn in my mind and remembered the beautiful sunsets as they splashed a rainbow of color behind the majestic hills.

"My grandparents had a place in the country. I always felt at peace when I visited them. I remember feeding apples to the young deer. They would come right up and take pieces out of my hand." I laughed. "Once I put a piece of fruit in my mouth, and this little buck brushed his soft lips against mine to take the treat. I giggled and my granny hugged me to her big bosom. She called me her little apple dumpling."

"That's a wonderful memory. I can work with that. Okay, skootch on down the bed and close your eyes. Keep taking in deep breaths for me. I want you to bring back as many details as you can, as you think of your grandparent's home. Think about the smells, the sounds…."

CHAPTER SIX

Maya's meditation exercise had worked really well. I was having a beautiful dream about feeding a young buck, when I was startled awake. I heard crashing noises in the other room and wondered what the hell was going on. I froze in fear, thinking the government scientists had finally decided vacation was over.

"Shit. Shhh, shhh, settle down little one. I'm trying to help," I heard Maya say in her honey-dipped voice.

Crash, bang

Uh, oh, I knew those sounds. I'd probably conjured up something, and that very thing was causing a shitload of trouble. I jumped out of bed and ventured into the living room. The place looked like a burglar had tossed the joint. Lamps were turned over and the room was in a general disarray. Maya was attempting to corral a white-tailed deer.

In the animal's current state of panic, those tiny antlers protruding from his forehead could do some serious bodily harm.

The sliding-glass door was open wide, but the little deer wasn't getting the hint that he was definitely overstaying his welcome.

"Out," I yelled and pointed to the patio. A flash of brown streaked across the living room, as the furry creature bounded out the door and escaped into Maya's back yard.

Maya slammed the glass door shut and sighed.

I hung my head in shame. I braced myself for her words, knowing I was about to be thrown out on my ass. My last hope for a normal life had bounded out the door, just like the young buck.

"I suppose I made a rookie mistake last night," Maya said.

"Huh?"

"I know better than to guide a meditation with any kind of wild animal, especially with someone of your caliber. Next time you need to leave the deer out of the memory. You hungry?"

I imagine I was blinking my eyes, looking at her like she was a figment of my imagination. "Um…you're not tossing me out?"

She laughed. "Of course not, silly. That was my fault, not yours. We can clean up after we've had a hearty breakfast. I'm starved. Omelets, pancakes, French toast, or boring oatmeal, what's your pleasure?"

"Hmmm, my pleasure, now that is a loaded question." I'm only human. She was standing in front of me barely dressed in a pair of lacy underwear and not a single stitch of additional clothing. I wiggled my eyebrows for added effect.

She glanced down at her heaving breasts. "Oh dear, I suppose I'd better put on some more clothes."

"Oh, don't go to any trouble for me. I don't mind at all. It saves me the trouble of dreaming up that little fantasy. Although, in my dream it was a skimpy teddy." I waved my hand at her. "This look is soooo much better."

"I will take it very personally if you conjure up another woman while you're living with me, so don't even think of it," Maya threatened. "No one upstages me."

The pointed look she gave me left no room for interpretation. I filed that away and decided I'd better be the very best student I could be, lest I slip up and dream the same woman Syl had dealt with the other day.

†

Maya wouldn't let me fire up my rust bucket and insisted we take her much newer SUV over to Syl's house. I was directed to pull together some clothing and whatever else might make me more comfortable for my extended stay at her place. I had a slight twinge of guilt about leaving Satan. He would probably pout for days and ignore Syl. Eventually, he'd cozy up with her, if she was the only one around to fawn all over him. He was used to a lot of attention, because I had no one else to focus my adoration on.

I was easing more and more into my old self, as the medication dissolved completely from my system. Thankfully, I was in the cruising lane on a high, versus gearing down and sputtering into a low. I was sure Syl was going to raise a boatload of objections to the plan, but Maya didn't seem concerned at all.

After I climbed into her pristine car with the cushy leather seats, I looked out the window and realized that the ominous, black vehicle was empty. I glanced at Maya who had a very self-satisfied smile on her face.

"Where'd the G-man go?" I asked.

"Probably in the woods over there." She pointed to the lush greenery adjacent to her house. "I imagine he's peeing out his butthole right now." She laughed.

I decided right then that I never wanted to be on Maya's bad side. She had a very warped sense of humor, and I wouldn't relish feeling the brunt of her anger or disappointment. I shuddered in my seat, as I realized just how powerful a Dream Catcher Maya really was.

Maya clasped my hand and squeezed. "Heaven, you don't need to worry. I would never harm you or cause you distress. By the way, I wanted to compliment you on how you controlled your figment."

She smiled at me and I felt all warm and tingly, but I was confused. The adolescent deer I'd dreamed about had left a small wake of destruction.

"Um…I didn't control anything. Sure, the little guy was cute, but he still broke a bunch of things in your house. I can't believe you aren't angry about that."

"I'm talking about when you woke up and ordered him outside. I didn't have to teach you how to do that. It came naturally. Have you been able to control your creations before?"

I shrugged. "Not really. In the past, the ones that have caused harm usually freaked me out too much and I would kind of freeze. I guess this time, since it wasn't some ferocious beast, I reacted with the first thought that popped into my head. Out."

Maya put the SUV in gear and pulled out into the street. "Hmmm." She glanced over at me.

"Hmmm, what? Is that a good hmmm or a bad hmmm?" I was squirming under her scrutiny.

She turned her focus back on the road. "Well, it appears as though you have the raw talent and the sky's the limit on your ability to control things. Since you were able to direct the small buck without any training from me at all, I have no doubt about your aptitude for surpassing my skills."

I folded my arms across my chest and slumped into the seat. "Doubtful. I am a world class fuck-up. Always have been and always will be."

Maya nodded and I thought she was agreeing with me, until she blurted out, "Okay that settles it. We need to do a major rehaul on your self-esteem and perspective. That will be the first lesson. You, Heaven, are a rare and beautiful treasure. I will get you believing that before we are done."

†

I wasn't sure what we would encounter when we reached Syl's place. I didn't consider it my home, because I was just staying there as a result of Syl's profound guilt over her participation in the government's less-than-ethical dream program. Still, Syl could be very protective. She'd already expressed her discomfort over the suggestion of me living with Maya for a few months.

I didn't think too much about using my key unannounced, but I immediately wanted to turn back around and pick my shit up later. There were loud moans of pleasure coming from Syl's bedroom.

Maya gently pushed me inside. "Oh, I am so glad. I wasn't looking forward to a minibattle with Syl. It sounds like she'll be too occupied to cause a riff. Don't mind us, Syl, we'll be in and out," she called out.

I cringed and prepared myself for cyclone Syl. "Um, best not to poke that bear."

Maya chuckled. "You worry too much. I might have included a bit of suggestion in my command. It's a simple parlor trick I'll teach you. When the subject is already inclined to obey, it's a whole lot easier to accomplish. Chop, chop, Heaven, my suggestion doesn't have long staying power."

I scurried into my bedroom and began to toss various items of clothing into a duffel bag. I didn't have a whole lot, so it was easy to choose what I would take. I grabbed almost everything in my drawers and closet, then added my grooming items from the tiny guest bath. The bag looked pregnant, as I yanked on the zipper and managed to close it over the large bulge in the center.

Satan jumped on the bed and looked up at me. He had a pitiful expression on his face as if he was asking me, *Mom, are you abandoning me?*

Maya was absently petting my cat and cooing at him. "Oh, what a pretty boy you are."

While Maya gave my cat attention, I stood in my bedroom wondering if I should take the mementos in the jewelry box that sat on the dresser. Syl's disheveled head appeared in the doorway. Darla stood behind her with a slight grin on her face.

"Hiya, Syl," I said.

Syl frowned. "Don't you think it would be prudent to talk about this before you go traipsing off with a relative stranger?"

Maya calmly answered, "Darla has known me for a very long time, so by extension, I am no stranger, Syl. I know you're worried about your friend, but this is the perfect solution. I need concentrated time to help Heaven, and you need quality time with Darla. It's a win, win."

"What about her dream manifestations? How do you plan to control them without medication? I know how to handle Heaven, you are hardly qualified to deal with her, uh…"

"Gifts?" Maya narrowed her eyes.

"That isn't the word I would use," Syl answered.

Darla ran her hand down Syl's arm. "Hon, we talked about this last night. I trust Maya. She knows what she's doing. You have to let go. I know you feel responsible for what happened, so let Maya do what she does best. Your solutions haven't been working all that well. You have to admit that no one is benefiting from the chemical therapy you've developed."

"If she would just take her meds on a consistent basis…"

I exploded at that point and interrupted Syl, "I'm not me when I take your drugs. I hate them and I hate myself. Please, Syl, don't fight this."

Syl hung her head. "I'm so sorry, Heaven, I never meant for…"

She started to choke up, and I crossed the room to hug her. After we separated, I assured her, "I know, and I don't blame you. Really, I don't. Now go back and get naked with your woman."

She pulled me in for another hug and squeezed. "Can you at least update me? Daily. I want daily briefings on your progress. I promise to take care of the furry beast."

I swiped my hand over Satan's silky fur. "You be good for Auntie Syl." He rolled over on his back, and Syl rubbed his belly. He'd be fine. I doubted he would even miss me.

†

The ride back to Maya's house was devoid of chatter. I felt bad about yelling at Syl and was desperately trying not to let my poisonous notions of dread infiltrate my flawed beliefs.

Maya was humming to the radio. She reminded me of a sunflower growing tall and reaching to the heavens. She was everything bright and yellow. Almost nothing seemed to sour her mood. The only time I ever saw a dark side was whenever she noticed the government agents assigned to tail me.

After I'd put away all my measly belongings in the guest bedroom, Maya appeared in the doorway. The sunshine came through the living room window at just the right angle, and she looked like an angel with the light emanating off of her.

"Shall we have a bit of fun, now that you're all settled?" She quirked her lips into a mischievous smile.

I wiggled my eyebrows. "What kind of fun did you have in mind?"

Maya laughed. "Not that kind of fun. Tell me about your passions. What stirs your interest?"

I shrugged. It had been a long time since I'd done anything besides, eat, sleep, or watch TV. Since leaving the

47

institution, I kept a low profile and rarely ventured out. "A movie?" I tentatively suggested. It seemed a safe bet.

"Oh, Heaven, you can do better than that. Let's go zip lining."

I gulped. "Zip lining?"

"Bungee jumping?" she offered.

"Are those my only two choices?"

Maya placed her finger against her cheek. "Well, I don't think we could arrange for sky diving. It's too late in the day, and I don't have any connections for that activity. I suppose we could consider hot air ballooning, but that recent accident with the power lines was so unfortunate. I don't suppose you want to try that just yet."

I looked into her eyes and realized she wasn't joking. My heart began to beat loudly in my chest; I hadn't realized what a scaredy-cat I was until that precise moment. "Um, I guess I'll take door number one please, zip lining." *How dangerous can that really be?*

"It's not dangerous at all, Heaven. Nowadays they rarely have accidents."

Her assurances did not make me feel better. "How, uh…high up will we go?"

"I know just the place. I've seen a five-year-old handle it like a pro. Tomorrow, maybe we can go to this hang gliding place I know." Maya had a twinkle in her eye.

"That was a joke, right?" I quivered.

She chuckled. "Yeah. I'm kidding. I figured I might have to start with baby steps."

"Is this part of the training?"

"Yes, Heaven. I like to combine fun with my training. It helps ease a person into the trust that is required for the more intensive parts…"

Oh holy hell, what in the world did I get myself into?
"Okay," I reluctantly agreed.

I jumped when Maya clapped her hands together. "Fabulous, we're going to have such a good time. Just wait, you'll see. Now chop, chop, we'd better get going while we have all this wonderful sunshine."

I'm sure my smile was anemic.

†

I looked down to the lush forest, as I dangled about fifteen feet away from the platform that I was supposed to reach at the end of the zipline. I'd followed the instructions to a T. The tall dude with the soul patch was pulling himself down the line to grab me and bring me to where Maya was grinning like a fool. I felt stupid hanging with the harness bunched up close enough to my crotch that I thought I might get a clit wedgie. That was definitely not my idea of a good time.

When my feet touched the platform, I complained loudly, "I tucked into a ball, just like you said. How come I didn't make it all the way?" I'd addressed my question to Jeremy or Jason or Justin—some J name I couldn't remember, because I suck at names.

"Cause you don't got enough meat on your bones." He scratched his soul patch. Screw it I would just call him Patch.

Maya moved her eyes up and down my body. "You are kind of a petite little thing. I had no trouble making it all the way. Isn't this a blast?"

I glanced at the cluster of thorny bushes at least forty feet below where I stood. I knew I would fall to my death without ever tasting the beautiful Maya. "Um…sure. How many more of these lines are left again?"

Patch chuckled. "You're not afraid of heights, are you? We only lose the occasional tourist. Just don't make any sudden moves while I'm unclipping you. It's such a mess when we have to scrape someone off the trail below." He poked me. "Hey, just kidding. This is totally safe."

I should have puked on his stupid, nineties, soul patch. I wanted to yell at him that the damn thing went out of fashion years ago and he should sport a man bun instead.

Maya scooted next to me and whispered, "Heaven, if you want this to be the last one we do, just say the word."

"Nah, I'm good. But if I fall, you're picking the thorns out of my ass, and I expect extra special attention on that part of my body." I grinned at her.

The very last zipline was the longest and the fastest. I allowed myself a certain amount of freedom to enjoy the ride, without thinking about how far up I was as I careened down the line and hit the final platform. It was all worth it when Maya kissed my cheek, and her hot breath hovered over my ear as she whispered, "Your smile reveals the truth. This last zip was just a tiny bit fun. Should we go back to the front of the line and do it all over again?" Her deep-throated chuckle sent vibrations up and down my body.

"Only if I get a real kiss at the end."

Thankfully, we did not go to the start of the line as she suggested, and when my stomach grumbled, she proposed an out of the way café down the road.

We were laughing when we exited Adventureland, but her mirth quickly ceased when she glanced to her right. I spotted the dark sedan with the tinted windows.

"Clearly, my suggestions weren't strong enough," she muttered.

"It's okay." I tried to calm her burgeoning fury. "Mostly they just follow me."

I watched in awe, as she marched over and pounded on the window with a crisp sense of purpose. "You've been warned. The next time, a toilet seat won't be the only thing you'll dread seeing. If you leave right now, I'll go easy on you. If not…" Maya didn't bother to finish. She stood frozen in the gravel road for nearly thirty seconds and appeared to be in some kind of trance.

My mouth was probably hanging open when she crossed the path and looped her arm in mine. "The stupid assholes will never learn. He'll be scratching his privates for hours, while he periodically pulls his pants down checking for fleas, bedbugs, spiders or whatever his mind conjures up as the most heinous of creepy crawly things."

"How do you do that?"

"I'll teach you, don't worry." I glanced back just in time to see the man in the car jump out and yank down his pants.

CHAPTER SEVEN

It wasn't so much that I didn't enjoy spending time with Maya, but I failed to see how the last couple of days had taught me anything. The meditation exercise did help me fall into a calm sleep. I'd had an uneventful night of dreams, as I frolicked through a field of wildflowers without any furry creatures joining my peaceful moment with nature.

I woke early to hushed whispers. I crept to the door and carefully cracked it open. Maya looked agitated. The low tones of her voice floated in the air, and I could tell she was trying to be careful and quiet.

"I told you. I have it handled. These things take time. Don't you take that tone of voice with me… She doesn't know… Okay, okay…"

I took a step back, startled by what I was hearing. Stupid, that's what I was, stupid. I was being played. I'd let a beautiful woman cloud my judgment. I stumbled on one of my shoes and made a noise. Maya quickly pivoted and probably saw the door cracked open. I didn't know who Maya was working for, but I was determined to find out. I'd play along with her little game until I learned what I needed to know.

The padding of her feet drew near, and I scrambled back to bed pulling the sheet over myself as I pretended to still be asleep.

I heard the humor in her voice, as she pushed open the door and said, "I know you overheard me and are now pretending that you're still asleep. Nice effort, by the way. It's not what you think, but I don't expect you're going to believe that." Maya sighed. "I suppose I'll just have to earn your trust, but I can't give you all the answers you need at this time. You'll just have to be patient."

I shifted in bed and glared at her. I'm not sure if it was a product of what the government did to my psyche or just fundamentally who I was, but I sometimes found that my train of thought often left the station without me. "Don't count your chickens. I'll never trust you." So much for playing along and trying to learn her game.

Maya just laughed. Laughed. Like I was some kind of petulant child.

I threw off the covers to the bed and stood with my hands on my hips, daring her to continue laughing at me.

"Nice boi shorts. The smiley faces are cute."

I looked down at my underwear and crossed my arms over my naked upper body. I'd forgotten I wasn't wearing anything besides my happy panties. With all the dignity I could muster, I grabbed the T-shirt I'd tossed on the chair the night before and pulled it over my head. "You promised to teach me. I'm ready. No more stalling, or I'm outta here."

"Breakfast first. It's important to start the day with a hearty breakfast." Maya left the room with me standing there looking stupid in my underwear and crumpled T-shirt.

†

Sitting at the kitchen table, I played with my food, pushing it around on my plate as I slumped in the chair. I could feel the darkness begin to creep inside. I'd really wanted to believe in Maya's goodness, and now I knew it was all a lie.

"Stop acting like a petulant child," Maya chastised. "You think you know something, but you don't."

"Well then why don't you fill me in, oh wise one."

"Because it's not time, and that's not my role."

"I hate people who are cryptic. It's like we're in the middle of some stupid romantic intrigue movie and you're being evasive, because you have to drag this shit out so that all the people watching will stay engaged."

Maya bent over laughing. "You should be a script writer with your imagination. You must think I'm planning something really nefarious."

"Maybe not you, but I'll bet whoever you work for…"

Maya leaned forward and propped her elbows on the table. "Look, Heaven, I am not going to deny that you're important to us. It's why I offered to take you on as a client, but we're not the enemy here. We have a common adversary, the government," her voice dripped with vitriol.

I wasn't completely sold, but I did hear the genuine venom in her voice. She hated the people that had made me the monster I was, even more than I did. "Why can't you tell me more?"

Maya shrugged. "Let's just say that, at this time, you're a big risk. We're still learning about all the little tricks that have been used on you. Dr. Spartan has some very inventive ways to turn his subjects. They don't just let people leave, but here you are on your own, free as a bird. It makes us a little cautious. I can help you, but you're going to have to trust me. I can't let you spiral into one of your, uh, negative valleys."

I sat up and grinned at her. "Negative valleys? That's a new one. It's called depression. What? Scared of my big bad monsters, are ya? Well that's smart, because you should be." I glared at her.

Maya chuckled. "Heaven, you are a feisty one. I like it. No, I'm not scared of you or your monsters, but you haven't been very successful controlling your creations. I'd prefer to start with something easier. What can I do to tease you into a better mood?"

I wiggled my eyebrows. "Well…I can think of one thing…"

"Really, Heaven, so let me get this straight. You can sleep with me, even when you don't trust me?"

"I'm not sure there is anyone I trust. If I followed your logic, that you have to trust someone to have sex with them, I'd never get laid. As it is, I rarely get to scratch that itch anyway. Beggars can't be too choosey."

"Oh, Heaven, you've sequestered yourself away for far too long. As soon as you meet the other Catchers and Weavers, and we are able to gain some ground…I can't afford to let feelings get in the way of what has to be done, and I'm the only one who should be working with you…"

I almost thought she looked and sounded wistful. Then again, I couldn't really trust my perceptions. A distorted sense of reality was something that went along with my disease. Syl and everyone else who'd ever worked with me was always quick to point that out. "Yeah, right."

Maya clapped her hands together. "Let's do something you've always been dying to try but never had the courage. I know you didn't really want to go ziplining yesterday. You only agreed because you're too nice to assert yourself."

"It'll sound stupid to you."

"Try me." Maya's dimples made an appearance as she smiled at me.

"I've never had a pedicure, or a manicure for that matter."

"Done. I know just the place, and I'll have her throw in a mud mask."

I didn't know how to tell Maya that I didn't want someone smearing mud on my face. I only wanted the pedicure, but I didn't say anything.

Maya glanced at the plate of food I was playing with and waved her hand at the omelet. "Don't let the eggs get cold. I put my loving touch into that. It's extra fluffy, if I do say so myself. Eat up and we can head to Toes R Us."

"Toes R Us? That's just wrong." I took a bite of food just to humor her. She was right; the omelet was light and fluffy. In fact, it was downright delicious. I stopped my hunger strike and began shoving the scrumptious breakfast into my gob. Maya seemed pleased, and I had to admit I liked it when she smiled at me. That didn't mean I could trust her.

†

We drove up to this quaint, pink house. Pepto pink to be exact, with purple trim. I'd need a bottle of the chalky liquid after looking at this beastly color. *Who paints their house that color?*

Maya banged open the purple door and announced our arrival, "Hey, Raven, we're ready for the five-star service."

Raven? And I thought my name was hokey. My eyes roamed the place, as I took in the pastel-blue walls, the scent of patchouli, and a sweet-smelling incense that I couldn't quite place. A sixties revival was what came to mind. I focused on the crystals in the window sills, the new age music, and the smells that all screamed hippie-dippy crazies.

Sure enough, the beaded curtains were pushed aside by a woman whose flowered headband topped long, dark hair that reached the waist of bell-bottomed jeans. "Maya," she screamed. She grabbed Maya's face and planted a big smoocharoonie on her plump lips. I wanted to ask Maya if I could do that too. After all, weren't we all "family?"

"You look gorgeous," Maya remarked. "Are those chants still working?"

"Like a charm. Oh hey, I forgot to tell you—those crystals you asked me to find arrived the other day from Sedona. I can feel their power and energy. You must have something special planned for them."

Maya glanced over at me, and I shifted nervously.

The woman—whom I assumed was Raven, because nobody else seemed to be in the house—tilted her head and shifted her scrutiny to me. I felt like a bug under a microscope. "So, this is the one, huh. You didn't tell me how cute she is." She wiggled her eyebrows up and down. "Single too, right?"

Maya smacked her on the arm. "Stop it. We're here for a pedicure and a mask, no extras."

I piped up, "I like extras." She was attractive. Not as beautiful as Maya, but she had that curvy, seductive look going for her. So, sue me for fuck's sake, it had been a long time.

Raven didn't hesitate to gather me in her arms and smother me in an embrace, complete with a caress to my back that came dangerously close to my ass. After she released me from the hug that was a tad bit friendly for a stranger, she said, "Welcome, Heaven. I'm Raven and I'll be your hostess for the day. Since I'm a multitalented sort of gal, I'll be doing both the mask and the pedicure. Maya said you've never had either. Well…you're in for a treat, because I'm the best."

I wasn't about to forget the extras comment. I reminded her again, just in case it wasn't a joke. "Are the extras still on the table? Because I'd like to explore those possibilities."

Raven responded with a deep-throated chuckle. "You are absolutely adorable. I just want to eat you right up with a big old spoon. I don't think the kind of extras I offer are up your alley. You seem like the naïve type, but nothing wrong with a little sugar instead of the spice I usually excel at." She grabbed my face and planted the same kiss on me that she gave to Maya.

I wasn't expecting it and felt the flush travel to my face. "Oh, uh, is that the first extra?"

Maya pushed Raven away. "Go get the foot soak ready and stop making Heaven uncomfortable."

"I'm fine." I grinned.

Raven tossed me an impish smile before flitting off to the room behind the beaded curtain. Flitting seemed the only appropriate word to use, because the woman reminded me of some kind of faerie or magical creature, with a 1960s flair.

Maya narrowed her eyes. "Don't take Raven too seriously. She flirts with everyone."

"Wow, thanks. I know you didn't mean that to sound the way it came out. I know you intended it as a kind warning, but it felt like a dig," I replied with a touch of the anger I felt.

I softened my stance when it looked like Maya regretted her words. She was contrite when she tried to explain. "I'm sorry, Heaven. That didn't come out the way I wanted it to. It's just, you're special, and it sort of pissed me off that Raven treated you like she does everyone else. Besides, she's right about the scene she's into. It doesn't seem like something you would enjoy. She's just out for a good time, all the time, and you deserve so much more than her superficial advances."

"Maybe a frivolous affair is just what the doctor ordered. Ya know, it'll ease me into that emotional space you're angling for, like preparation for the work we need to do to prime me for controlling my dreams."

Maya shook her head. "I guess I can understand now how Syl responds to your…uh…escapades. Sex is not the answer. Come on, sit down over there on that chair, and Raven will bring the tub of water for your feet." Maya pointed to an empty chair.

"Sex is *an* answer, just never the one you killjoys will let me explore," I grumbled.

Maya chuckled, but didn't say anything else. I sat in the chair, waiting for my pampering.

CHAPTER EIGHT

I was looking at my painted toes and snuck a glance at Maya while she was making dinner. She must have thought I was overly enthralled with my new pedicure, because I caught her looking at me with a smile on her face. Busted. I was beginning to think she was just as interested in me as I was in her. She looked away quickly, but not before I caught her appraising me. From that point forward, I was on a mission to get Maya to join me for a little recreational sex. I still didn't trust her as far as I could throw her. *Ooh, throw her.* Suddenly, I got a vision of tossing her on the bed and holding her arms above her head, while I devoured every curvy inch of her body. I was imagining running my hands through her thick, chestnut hair.

"Uh, uh, uh, stop going there," she interrupted my pleasant thoughts.

"How do you do that?"

"Heaven, you are the most transparent person I know. You telegraph your thoughts so easily, a five-year-old could guess what you're thinking."

I crossed my arms and imagined I had a pout on my face worthy of a five-year-old.

"Don't pout," she said. "It mars your beautiful face."

"Well, if you'd stop flirting with me, I wouldn't have those thoughts."

Maya's deep laugh reverberated in the room. "Just stating the facts. You are exceptionally beautiful. Frankly, I'm surprised you aren't already paired."

I decided a change in topic was the only thing to do. "When are we going to start my training? It's not that I don't like your cooking, or our little daytime adventures, but…"

"You are an impatient one." She sighed. "We've already started, but we'll get more involved tonight."

"Oh goody, I like the sound of that." I didn't say this sarcastically. I really did want to start the more in-depth training. It was only a matter of time before my monsters arrived on the scene.

Maya stopped stirring the delicious sauce she was making and turned the stove dial to off. She reached into her pocket and pulled out her cell phone, then walked into her bedroom as she pressed the button to answer.

When she shut the door, I tiptoed over and plastered my ear against the solid wood. I could make out a few words.

"Tonight… Yeah, don't worry, I'll get her ready… No, I haven't…"

She must have walked further into her room or headed to the master bath, because I couldn't hear the rest. In the low rumbling of her voice, I thought I heard danger, but it could very well have been something else. When I heard her footsteps, I hightailed it back to my chair and tried to look innocent.

Maya narrowed her eyes at me before pulling the baked fish from the oven. I think she knew I'd tried to listen in on her conversation, but she didn't say a word.

"That looks good. Smells lovely too," I said.

She offered up her sexy smile. "Time to put your socks back on and come to the table. You can admire your pedicure later," she teased.

I grabbed the fluffy wool socks, pulled them over my feet, and scrambled over to the table. "I suppose I should be helping you out with dinner, but I'm kind of useless in the kitchen. Now in the bedroom…" I let my comment hang in the air.

"Temptress." She dished up the fish alongside rice and vegetables, then poured a generous amount of hollandaise sauce over everything.

It did look wonderful, and I dug in as soon as she sat. She looked at me expectantly.

"It's good," I mumbled through a bite of food.

She nodded and put a forkful in her own mouth, as her lips curved up in a small smile. After she finished chewing, she nonchalantly informed me, "Tomorrow we're going to travel to somewhere more remote, where I can provide the kind of intensive training needed to prepare you."

What the fuck? Oh, hell no. My thoughts raced; I wasn't about to go to some isolated location where she could starve me to death, so she could skin me alive and use my outer covering as a creepy coat. I admit, last week, I'd watched that old Jodie Foster movie, *Silence of the Lambs*. Still, Maya could be a crazy psychopath.

"I'd rather not," I squeaked.

Maya shook her head. "Heaven, your imagination, while admirable, is not very accurate. You're going to have to trust me. Have I done anything in the last two days to harm you in any way?"

"No," I hesitantly admitted.

"Well, okay then, it's settled. Tonight, I'll teach you the first trick, then we'll head out at sunrise tomorrow morning."

Resistance is futile. Okay, now I was remembering Seven of Nine and the Borg in one of my favorite TV series, *Star Trek: Voyager.* I watched entirely too much television, but the bottom line was that I didn't think I had an option at this point. Maya was going to shuttle me away to a secluded location and do God knows what to me. I only hoped I could charm my way out of anything drastic that would turn me into some weapon for the government.

†

I was sitting across from Maya in the lotus position, staring at a candle and thinking, *This exercise is the most ridiculous thing I've ever done.* The flame wavered in the air. *Strange, I don't feel a breeze.* Maybe it was my own deep breaths of exasperation that caused the mini torch to flicker.

"You're not concentrating," Maya chastised.

"I am too." I crossed my arms in defiance.

I was supposed to be imagining the candle was a menorah. *I'm not Jewish. How do I know what a menorah looks like?* I kept overthinking, trying to remember how many candles were in a menorah. I started thinking about all the different holidays in December and January. *Why don't the other holidays get much press? I should learn more about Kwanzaa.*

"It's not that hard, Heaven." Maya blew a raspberry. She was frustrated with me, I could tell. "Nine, there are nine candles in a menorah."

Well that answered *that* question for me. "Are there candles in a Kwanzaa celebration?"

"Yes, Heaven, there are seven candles in Kwanzaa."

"Well then why can't I focus on that? It would be easier to conjure seven versus nine," I countered.

"Whatever. Okay, you can think about the Kwanzaa kinara if that's easier for you."

I grinned. "Okay thanks." I stared at the single candle and tried. I really did try. *What other holidays use candles?* "Maya, maybe there's another holiday that has even less candles."

"Oh for shit's sake, Heaven. Stop overthinking this," she huffed. "All right, if you insist. How about you turn that into a luminaria? That should be simple enough."

I looked up into Maya's scowling face and hesitated before asking, "So what kind of bag were you thinking? Won't that cause a fire or something?"

Maya sighed. "Fine, just think of a candelabra with only three candles. Forget the luminaria. You're right, knowing you, it would burst into flames and light this place up too quickly for me to stop the madness. Just chant in your head, 'candelabra with three flames,' over and over."

"You don't have to be so snippy about it." I focused back on the single candle and did exactly as she suggested. I emptied my mind of all the other random thoughts and kept whispering over and over, "Candelabra with three flames."

Over the loudness of my thoughts, as I focused on those four words, I heard clapping. When I opened my eyes, I was surprised to find a beautiful, gold-plated candelabra, with three slender, purple candles. I grinned at my teacher.

"Okay, that's enough for tonight. I don't think we should push for more."

I silently agreed.

†

Honestly, I don't think it was my fault, what happened in the middle of the night. If Maya hadn't been secretive about that phone call, she wouldn't have had to use all her special tricks to send Seven of Nine back to never-never land.

My eyes popped open when I heard, "Resistance is futile."

Oh shit. I jumped out of bed and ran to the living room, where Maya was doing this humming thing. It looked like there was some invisible bubble around her that my apparition kept bumping into and bouncing off of.

I slammed my eyes closed and chanted, "Disappear, disappear, disappear." I wasn't sure why I did that. I guess I thought it might work.

Maya's shouts were muffled through whatever protective barrier she had erected. "No, Heaven, chant toy Borg, instead."

I tried it her way. I opened my eyes when I felt her gentle hands touch my shoulders. As I looked around, I couldn't find my hallucination. Maya pointed to the floor. A plastic figurine of Seven of Nine was laying on its side. I blinked a few times.

"Good job, Heaven. You're going to do well."

I plucked the toy from the floor and taunted, "Resistance is futile." The toy didn't answer. Yeah, I was the boss in this scene. I ventured a look toward the Catcher, to judge her reaction to my childish outburst.

I wasn't sure what to think. Maya didn't exactly seem upset by having to safeguard herself from my dream Borg, but she didn't seem overjoyed either. Something was up, and I got the feeling I wasn't going to like it.

"I'm sorry. If you made me take my meds, this wouldn't happen."

She tried to mask her sorrow…discomfort…pity. I wasn't quite sure what emotion overcame her face, but I wasn't buying it. "Meds are not the answer. I promise, everything will be all right."

"Okay, spill. What's the matter?"

"Go back to bed, Heaven. Tomorrow will be a long day for both of us."

CHAPTER NINE

Maya was uncharacteristically somber, as we drove along the bumpy path to wherever it was she planned to take me. She'd put her mojo on my shadow, who sat in his usual spot across the street from Maya's house. I didn't want to know what she'd done to him this time, and she wasn't in the mood to offer up any information. I did notice the lack of a tail, as we left her house.

The large tongue-and-groove cedar house nestled among the tall trees was downright awe inspiring. This was not some rundown shack in the woods. I didn't know a lot about houses, but I'd wager this one was easily in the millions.

"Whoa, who owns this place?" I asked.

"Someone who is very interested in meeting you."

"Did we just roll up to the Queen of the Catchers or something?" I joked.

Maya looked at me funny. "How'd you know?"

I squirmed in my seat. "I was kidding," I mumbled. "Hey you're not going to drop me off in this strange location with people I don't know, are you? Because, you know, if you are, I'm not staying."

Finally, Maya smiled at me and started to chuckle. "Oh really, Heaven, and where do you think you're going to go? You're in the middle of nowhere. Don't worry, I can stay for a little while, but Leah isn't going to be happy about that. She wanted some individual time with you."

"Look, I didn't make a deal with this Leah woman. I made it with you, and even though I don't trust you entirely, I don't even know her. What if she's ugly?"

I must have pissed her off with that comment, because she slammed the door and stood there with her hands on her hips, glaring at me. "Is that the only reason you agreed to work with me? Because you were hoping for a quick hop in the sack?"

I carefully emerged from the passenger's seat. "What? It was meant as a compliment. I think you're beautiful." I looked down at my feet. "You're fun and sweet to me. People aren't nice to me, they're mean," I whispered.

"We really do want to help, Heaven. You're going to have to start trusting someone, someday."

"I trusted Syl, and look where that got me. I suppose she did redeem herself in the end. Syl's the only other person who has ever been good to me. Please, don't leave me here with people I don't know," I pleaded.

Maya gathered me in her arms; her fingertips brushed my back, then wove into my hair, as I settled my head against her shoulder. Staring vacantly away toward the ground, I didn't even hear anyone approach.

"Maya, you made good time. Why haven't you brought Heaven inside and gotten her settled already?"

Maya seemed startled and abruptly released me from her embrace. "Sorry, Leah. Heaven was expressing some discomfort about being left with strangers."

"Nonsense. We are all sisters. Don't you feel the pull, the power of your dreams?"

I looked up, and a pair of dark, blue eyes were appraising me. I was riveted to those eyes. I felt like one of those helpless victims in an alien abduction. The tractor beam was pulling me in. I was prepared to go anywhere this woman wanted to take me. No questions asked. I was shaking my head in affirmation, as I stood transfixed to this exotic woman standing before us.

"Leah. Stop it," Maya said sharply.

"Don't tell me—"

Maya subtly shook her head.

Leah tore her eyes from mine. "Interesting."

It was almost as though I felt a pop in my head, and I blinked before scrutinizing the strange woman. She was wearing a loose-fitting pair of pants and tunic in a shimmering blue. Her leather sandals seemed comfortable, yet the designs etched into the leather gave them an otherworldly appearance. Leah's long, flowing hair was as striking as her eyes; spun gold shimmered in the sunlight. To describe Leah as attractive was an understatement.

When I focused on her lips, that's when I noticed it. She grinned at me. I was looking at a mirror image of Maya, down to the tiny dimples on both sides of her face. Leah was a blonde version of Maya. Same full mouth that made my heart go pitter patter when she smiled and the same high cheekbones. Their eyes were a little different, and Maya had chestnut-colored hair that cascaded down her shoulders, but I knew in an instant these two were somehow related to one another. I decided to ask Maya about that later, but after catching Leah's eye again, I wanted to go inside.

"I'm good. We can go inside," I said.

"I mean it, Leah, you don't have to do that," Maya warned.

Leah shrugged, then turned around and began walking up the stone steps and into the elegant house. "Force of habit."

†

When I stepped over the threshold of the home, I felt the subtle richness of the wood and stone. The two different textures swirled together in a perfect combination of rustic elegance. I could tell every single detail was designed to create a space of serenity and beauty. I made a beeline for the floor-to-ceiling windows and couldn't believe what I was seeing. The estate had a waterfall that emptied into what they probably called a pond. To me, it was a fucking lake.

"Do you like water, Heaven?" Leah asked.

Somehow Leah had snuck up behind me. I could smell her sweet scent, as I felt her warm breath on my neck. "Uh, yeah, sure."

"The pond is for swimming, but if you prefer a soak, the hot tub is lovely." Leah pointed to another pool of water surrounded by natural stone, where steam hovered in the air.

"Okay," I answered.

Leah brought her fingertips down my arm, and I felt a shiver travel up and down my spine. I wasn't sure if Leah was trying to impress me or just make me feel comfortable, but I didn't care. I got the distinct impression that I was going to enjoy my stay here very much, even if the training was hard. I'd never felt special before. The most I'd experienced was grudging admiration for my "special talents," but even then, the scientists managed to treat me like a lab rat or a tool they manipulated to further their agenda. Spartan always treated me with utter revulsion. Leah made me feel like I was something extraordinary. It wasn't anything overt that she did, but I felt a bit of joy whenever she looked at me.

"Am I the only one here that you are planning on training?" The place was too large and exquisite to cater to just one person. Yet, I wanted to be the only one on the receiving end of Leah's special touch.

"Would you like to be the only one," she purred.

"Oh brother, you just can't help yourself, can you?" Maya grumbled.

I glanced at Maya, and she rolled her eyes. Sibling rivalry crossed my mind as an explanation for the strange interaction between Maya and Leah, and I blurted out my question, "Are you sisters?"

Maya and Leah looked at one another, and Leah answered, "Same father, but different mothers." She frowned, and it sounded like she wanted to spit out the word father because it was so distasteful.

I was intrigued. "Sounds like you don't like your dad."

"He's a bastard who will someday get the karma he deserves," Leah responded.

"We haven't had lunch yet, so I hope you have something prepared," Maya interrupted.

Leah slid her arm through mine. "Of course, I have the dining room all set up. Raven and a few others are hanging out in the entertainment room, waiting for you to arrive."

Leah started to lead me to another part of the massive house, and I wondered about this entertainment room. "What's in your entertainment room?"

"Oh, a movie theatre."

I shuddered, remembering the kind of movies Spartan had made me watch.

"They are never those kind of movies," Leah responded to my thoughts. "The pool table and other stuff that appeal to a certain kind of person are in the game room. I never quite understood the attraction, but some of our charges gush over that room, while the romantics prefer the entertainment center, and still others gravitate to the indoor spa or the outdoor tranquility center."

"Just how big is this place? You have more stuff than a five-star hotel," I blurted out.

Leah waved her hand in the air. "It's only fifteen thousand square feet. We've almost grown out of it, but we need a few more cash infusions before considering a move."

"Holy shit, fifteen thousand feet!" I turned to Maya. "How come you live in a hovel?"

Maya harrumphed. "My place is not a hovel and is perfectly comfortable to me."

"Maya has no vision, which is why I lead the Dream Fulcrum and not her," Leah calmly explained.

Maya had a strange look on her face that I couldn't quite decipher. I had the distinct impression that all was not as it appeared on the surface.

I decided to go back to the previous comment about Raven and the others. "So, who else is joining us for lunch? I guess I'm not the only person undergoing training."

"We have three others but none as talented as you, Heaven. I will personally be responsible for your training, in conjunction with Maya of course."

Maya raised her eyebrow. "Is that so? I thought you were taking over the training."

Leah smiled brightly. "I've decided we will do it together, since you have already established a rapport with Heaven and she seems quite taken with you, even though you haven't used all your skills on her."

Maya's jaw clenched. "I didn't bring any clothes or anything else, because I didn't know I was staying."

"We have everything you need, don't worry little sister."

"I don't suppose there is any room for negotiation here?"

I watched the two sisters ping pong back and forth. I was a little disappointed and hurt that Maya didn't want to stay, and apparently, I had a hard time keeping my feelings under wraps.

Maya's eyes bored into me. Her regret looked sincere. "I'm sorry, Heaven, I don't mean to suggest that I'm not interested in helping or seeing this through to the end. I was just surprised by the turn of events. My sister is a bit rash and spontaneous sometimes. It is hard to adjust to."

I wasn't unhappy about Maya joining with her sister to train me, and I knew I'd been kind of a shit to her earlier, suggesting that I didn't trust her, but I was confused about her reaction to this sudden change of plans. Perhaps I wasn't ready to verbalize it to Maya or her sister, but I did trust Maya. She made me feel all happy inside and instilled a sense of peace and calm that was incredibly difficult to achieve with someone like me.

"I only want you to stay if that's what you really want to do. Otherwise, don't do me any favors," I said more harshly than I felt.

Leah glared at Maya. "Of course she's staying." Her tone left no room for interpretation. It was an order.

I jerked away from Leah and stopped in my tracks. With my arms folded in defiance, I turned to face Maya. "Don't tell her what to do. She stays only if she wants to, or I'm not cooperating." I was seething. Most of my life people had been telling me what to do, and I hated it. I didn't want that for Maya. She smiled at me and brought her fingertips to my cheek with a butterfly caress.

"Heaven, there is nowhere else I'd rather be." Maya shocked me with a brief brush of her lips against mine.

Leah scrutinized us for a couple of seconds. "Come on, everyone is waiting, and I am suddenly famished." Her voice hadn't lost the commanding tone.

I tried not to gawk at the astonishingly beautiful artwork peppered throughout the house. Sculptures, paintings, drawings, mediums I didn't have a name for—all women. They weren't just individual women, but women together in various stages of eroticism. The collection was a lesbian's wet dream. I wondered if the other trainees would appreciate the art as much as I did.

"Holy shit." The words slipped out of my mouth before I could edit my impulsive reaction to what could only be described as a banquet hall in the middle of the residence.

Four eager faces looked up from the table they were sitting at, as a sexy Latina woman in a short maid's outfit was setting down steaming bowls of aromatic soup. I could smell the blend of spices the minute we reached the threshold of the room.

"I'm not letting some woman serve me. That's degrading to her." I refused to play in the elegant sandbox laid before me. I wanted no part of this rich person's fantasy.

Leah and Maya both laughed, and it was the first time I considered them in agreement on anything.

"Oh Jimena doesn't work for Leah. She's Raven's…hmmm…how shall I put this?" Maya began. "Raven and Jimena enjoy a special relationship. Trust me, she's getting out of this every bit as much as she's putting in."

Raven swatted Jimena lightly on her rear and chuckled. "Now go sit in the corner, while we finish lunch. If you've been a very good little maid, you'll get exactly what you deserve."

"Yes ma'am." Jimena bowed her head, but not before her hooded eyes met mine and I could see a tiny curve to her lips.

"Stop checking out Heaven," Raven barked.

"Sorry, Raven." Jimena sat in a chair with her hands clasped in her lap.

I wondered how Raven could justify snipping at Jimena after flirting shamelessly with me in her shop the other day. All of a sudden, I didn't like Raven and whatever little games she played. I saw a whole new side of her that she hadn't revealed when she'd done my pedicure.

Jimena was a fresh fascination. I couldn't help myself; I snuck a peak in her direction and saw that very short uniform ride up her thighs giving me a glimpse of her lacy, black underwear. I looked away quickly, when I registered the smirk on her face before she met Raven's disapproving glower from the table.

The glare of the spotlight focused on my head, as several of the women unabashedly checked me out. Leah pointed at the women at the table. She started with the woman on the far left, who resembled the gymnastic darling, Marylou Retton, with her pixie haircut. "Brenda, Star, Francine, and Deidre, meet Heaven."

I giggled as I thought about the comic book character, Brenda Starr, and wondered if Brenda and Star were a couple. They were seated close to one another and I saw Brenda whisper in Star's ear. Star probably didn't like what she heard, because she looked pissed.

I raised my hand and waved at the group of women. Brenda winked with a come-hither nod, as she gave me a little wave.

Maya touched my shoulder and gently led me to an open seat, where a bowl of soup sat on a plate of fine china. I waited for Leah and Maya to take the empty seats on my right and left. Although the table was beautifully set with crystal, china, and cloth napkins, the guests, apparently, did not stand on ceremony. They were already slurping their spoons, as they devoured the soup.

I waited until the two sisters picked up their spoons, before I tasted the creamy soup. Oh my Goddess, the golden treasure slid down my throat, after tantalizing every single taste bud and nerve on its journey to my stomach. The sweet tasting butternut squash soup was, indeed, fit for a queen. I tasted a hint of garlic, honey, and ginger, but wondered what other spices were in this culinary masterpiece.

"Lavender," Leah said. I looked at her and must have had a puzzled expression on my face. "It's the ingredient you're searching for. Sometimes chefs will add tarragon, but I prefer lavender with the ginger cream on top. Don't you agree it gives that special touch? I do declare, the soup is not unlike you, my dear Heaven. Something woven into the stock which truly makes it stand out."

"Lost my napkin," Brenda announced, as she proceeded to slide down in her chair and crawl under the table. I jumped when I felt her hand slide up my leg and almost reach my crotch. That started a chain reaction. My water glass tipped over, and Maya jumped up when the cold water dribbled on her lap. Francine and Deidre began to guffaw loudly, after peeking under the table.

"Behave yourself, Brenda," Leah ordered.

I grabbed my napkin and tried to towel off Maya, who turned a lovely shade of red. Brenda's head popped back up, and she grinned at me while I continued to pat down Maya.

"It's okay, a little water never hurt anyone." Maya sat back in her chair, and I tried to soak up the rest of the water on the table.

"Leave it. Jimena, a little help here," Raven barked.

I wondered where that hippie-dippy person had gone. Raven's whole attire had seemed the exact opposite of a dominatrix when she was in her shop.

"Oh yes, right." Jimena scurried away.

I slumped back into my seat and looked around, trying to make sense of everything. I might be a little nuts, but these women were all cray-cray. I'd fallen into a lesbian commune of the rich and infamous. Normally, being in the presence of attractive lesbians would make my spirits rise, but I was afraid I was about to learn a whole new passel of bad habits.

"Brenda's a sweetheart, but she's a sex addict. Along with trying to teach her how to control her dreams, we're trying to provide some education on tamping down her pregnant libido," Leah nonchalantly explained.

"So, stay away, newbie. She was doing fine 'til you showed up." Star glared at me. Deidre and Francine started cackling again.

"Enough." Leah captured each person's eyes for a second or two.

Something shimmered in the air, and the four women abruptly returned to their soup. *What did I just see?* My thoughts were interrupted when Jimena came back into the room and paused with the towel in her hand. She seemed to take in the scene before blotting the table. I thought her efforts to sop up the spill were moot. The water had already absorbed into the tablecloth, but she continued to nervously pat the table.

"That will be all, Jimena. You can bring the next course now. There will be plenty of time to play with Raven after lunch. We'll start training at three. Finish your soup, Heaven."

I blinked once, then bowed my head to finish the soup and do my best not to capture anyone's eyes. I couldn't resist a side glance at Maya, who offered a sad smile.

I wasn't looking forward to training with this group, but it didn't seem like I had a choice in the matter. At least I'd enjoy gourmet food while staying in the looney bin with the rest of the crazies. I simply needed to avoid eye contact with anyone and I'd be fine.

CHAPTER TEN

Everyone was sitting quietly in a circle. I felt that strange buzz in my head again and sat transfixed, hanging on every word that Leah uttered. I think everyone else was gobsmacked by her as well, because no one was acting out as she prepared us for the next few weeks.

"I'm going to confess to using a small amount of my talent at the start of our training. Once we get into the swing of things, I will slowly release control. Each of you will be allowed complete freedom to grow your skill," Leah began.

"Can we at least get to know each other a little better before all the hard work begins? I don't think it's a big surprise that I traded sexual favors for my freedom, but I'd kinda like to know how everyone else escaped and why they aren't trying very hard to bring us back." Brenda crossed her legs and smiled at me. "I know Star's story, but I heard

Heaven was a real loss to them. How come the black suits didn't follow you to lesbian heaven?"

I glanced at Maya, wondering if I should answer. I was about to toss in my theory, when I had a sudden desire to keep those thoughts to myself. I suspected Leah was impacting my ability to think and feel, but for some reason, I didn't mind.

"Let me provide a brief lesson about our enemy. All of you here are second or third generation Weavers and Catchers. The first batch they experimented on didn't work out too well for them. The unintended consequences of their drug therapy led to a blatant disregard for human life. They terminated the subjects for being far too unstable. Second generation did not fare very well either. The government wasn't able to prevent a high percentage of the clever subjects from taking their own lives, along with several scientists."

"I never wanted to off myself, but I wouldn't have minded sending a few of my special apparitions on a rampage. Maya found a sympathetic scientist, and they arranged for my transfer to Leah's retreat," Francine explained.

"Leah put her mojo on a few of the asshats who were getting ready to grab Jimena, then brought her to stay with me until Leah was ready to train a new batch of Weavers. I've been away from them for some time now. I'm one of the lucky second-generation Weavers who didn't take a nose dive into depression," Raven added.

I waited for Francine or Deidre to fill in the blanks and tell their stories, but nothing was forthcoming.

"We will start an exercise together, then the Weavers and Catchers will separate. Maya will take the Catchers, and I will work with the Weavers," Leah announced.

Maya frowned. "I usually take the Weavers, why the change?"

Leah shrugged. "I believe we have a special consideration that we've not had to deal with previously. Don't let your personal feelings get in the way."

"I'm—"

"Enough." Leah held up her hand. "I've made my decision."

I wasn't empathic and couldn't read anyone's mind, but it wasn't difficult to see Maya's frustration and anger.

"Raven and Maya, you take Jimena, Star, and Deidre. Raven, no games with Jimena, please, just work with her like you would any other trainee," Leah warned.

Raven glared at Leah. "As if. I'm not a novice at this."

"Just remember the end game." Leah turned her charming smile back at the remaining players.

Half of the group stood up and followed Maya and Raven to places unknown. The house was so large, I suspected they could scream their heads off and we wouldn't hear them if they went to some far-off corner of the massive compound. That's what it was starting to feel like to me, some kind of posh, military compound. With that mental picture latched onto my brain, I was sure to conjure up some scary, paramilitary dude tonight.

"We'll start with something small, perhaps a candle," Leah interrupted my dark train of thought.

"What's with the stupid candle thing?" I muttered.

Leah's eyes shifted to me, and they were like two small ice chips. "Heaven, would you care to share with the rest of the group?"

I could have sworn her eyes were dark blue before, but they'd suddenly become the blue frost of an iceberg. I imagined a flash of red on the edges; it was downright terrifying.

"Um, no."

"Good, then I will expect no further interruptions to the lesson today."

"No ma'am." I dropped my head, feeling like a chastised child.

For the next two hours, we repeated the exercise that Maya and I had already practiced. We'd thoroughly explored the description and number of candles, so I was free to concentrate on performing the task as Leah directed. I felt like a star pupil, because I produced all nine candles and managed to complete the task before Francine or Brenda had settled on their floor pillows.

†

Leah was so pleased with our progress that she let us explore on our own until we were expected to return to the dining room at six thirty. I scurried away quickly, before Brenda could catch up with me, and returned to the room they'd assigned to me. I felt a little more settled when I learned that Maya was in the adjoining room.

I wanted to check out the stone pool and the hot tub that I'd spied when I first arrived. I didn't have a swimsuit, but I figured a tank top and a pair of shorts would suffice. I stuck my head outside the bedroom door and looked right and left.

I didn't want to run into Brenda. She scared me more than Leah. I talked a big game and hadn't had sex in a while, but Brenda was not the type of person I was interested in tangling with. Besides, Star seemed like a jealous sort.

I tiptoed my way to the back yard and carefully opened the glass door. A sense of peace and well-being immediately affected me, and I dipped my foot into the water cascading down from the waterfall.

I was delighted to find the pond was a heated pool, and selected one of the flotation devices so I could paddle my way to the hot tub. I found and pressed the small button embedded into one of the stones, and a swirl of bubbles surrounded my body. I leaned my head back against the smooth stone and let the whirlpool take me to another place. I was so engrossed in my solo journey that I didn't hear anything but the bubbling water.

When a wave of new energy reached me through the pool, I opened my eyes and watched Maya's graceful form, as she swam through the pond. Droplets of water glistened on her body, and I felt a wave of arousal when she emerged in the small pool of hot water and slicked back her dark hair.

"Do you mind if I join you?"

I paused, because her beauty rendered me temporarily speechless, then I blurted out, "Wow, you are exquisite." With her hair slicked back, I could see her finely chiseled features, including her luminous green eyes.

Maya blushed. "How'd you manage to slip away from Brenda?"

I laughed. "I don't know, other than checking out the hallway before sneaking out to the pool. Maybe she doesn't like water."

"It is a little chilly for a swim. I'm surprised you braved the winter weather. How did you know the pool was heated?"

"I didn't. I just felt the pull of the waterfall and figured, as soon as I entered the hot tub, it would be fine."

"Mmmm. This place is almost sacred and provides me with the tools to gather perspective when I find myself trying to solve a problem."

Maya had sidled close to me, and we sat side by side on the sculpted stone benches. I had an overwhelming desire to touch her, but I resisted. I wanted to know what predicament was causing her so much angst. I could see it mapped all over her face.

"What's your dilemma? Maybe I can help."

Maya got a strange look on her face and finally responded, "I doubt that the source of my conflict can help me work through my options."

"What?"

"Never mind, I've said too much already. We should enjoy the healing powers of the pool," she said.

I didn't have the energy for riddles, so I slouched down into the water, until my entire body was enveloped in the protective warmth, then laid my head back on the smooth stone. I hadn't intended on falling asleep. I was in a good mood. In fact, I hadn't devolved into one of my severe depressive moments since the last night at Syl's.

†

I awoke to the sound of laughter and turned my head in the direction of the welcome intrusion. Some of the Catchers and Weavers were standing just outside the sliding-glass

84

door, with their arms around their bodies in an apparent attempt at keeping warm. Maya and a few others were in the hot tub. Maya's eyebrow was raised, and Brenda was clapping her hands. Leah had an impassive expression; I couldn't tell if she was angry, happy, frustrated, or amused.

Finally, I swiveled my head around and saw what everyone was focused on. To the right of the pool, a very naked woman was sliding up and down a pole that appeared to emerge from the stone patio.

Oh shit.

"Not that she isn't a welcome addition for this group, but it is a bit nippy out here. The poor woman is probably freezing her very nice ass off," Maya said.

I had to agree, she did have a very nice ass. Perhaps not as appealing as Maya's, since I'd caught a glimpse of hers when she dove into the pool and her globe broke the surface for a brief moment.

"So, what do you expect me to do? Order her into the house and wrestle up some clothes?" I asked.

"You need to send her back into your head, but that is a more advanced skill, similar to controlling your creations." Maya sighed. "I'll take care of her."

"Can't we just wait until she dissipates on her own? I think the gals are enjoying her," I said.

"I sure am," Brenda interjected.

"Enough," Leah barked. She glanced at the pole dancer, and one second later, my apparition and her pole had disappeared.

Irritated. Yep, now I recognized Leah's expression.

"Aw, you're no fun," Brenda mumbled.

"Dinner will be served in fifteen minutes, and I expect everyone to be on time."

The women standing at the sliding-glass door went back into the house, and I looked at Maya who shrugged. I figured I probably wouldn't have time for a shower, but after dog paddling back with my floaty, maybe I would be able to dry my hair. Reluctantly, I began to kick my legs through the warm water. I felt a mild disturbance, as Maya matched my journey back to the other side, stroke by kick. I felt her body next to mine, and there was a kind of energy vibration that I didn't quite understand but welcomed.

CHAPTER ELEVEN

While at dinner, it felt like someone had wrapped chains around my emotions and stuffed a sock in my mouth, preventing any verbalization of the random thoughts floating around in my head. I was beginning to understand how powerful Leah was. There wasn't any doubt in my mind she was tightly controlling the dinner conversation.

Brenda wasn't acting out, and the rest of the women were polite and respectful. Jimena had joined the group and was sitting at the table wearing a pullover and baggy pair of jeans instead of her maid's outfit. The only person who appeared to have any color whatsoever was Maya.

She sat next to me, and her energy vibrated off her in angry waves. I suppose she couldn't hold it in any longer.

Maya stood and glared at Leah. "Leah, stop it. Release them, or I will go in and sever your hold. You don't have to control every little minute of the day."

"Sit down, Maya. You're making a spectacle of yourself. Shall I remind you who is in charge here and for a very good reason?"

"It was an error in judgment that you know I regret." Maya slumped back in her chair.

I could feel my emotions seeking an outlet, attempting to slither from the cuffs. I wanted to stride to Maya's defense. Suddenly, something felt like a pop in my head, and I pushed away from the table, "I'm done here. Mental manipulation is nearly as bad as an unwelcome shot in my ass. You want my cooperation? Stay the fuck out of my head. I don't want you training me. I want Maya."

Leah's eyes went wide, and the corner of Maya's lip barely turned up.

"You broke the psychic bind," Leah stated incredulously, as she locked eyes with Maya. "Very well. You may train with Maya. I will grant your request, since the two of you seem to have a rapport that will ultimately serve our end game. Don't screw this up, Maya. Heaven is the key. I don't need to remind you of that."

"That's another thing. I'm sick and damn tired of you two talking in riddles. You want me to help with something, well then you'd better give me all the details. I've never been a good soldier. I'll not follow any directive blindly. I gotta believe in the cause or no dice. *Capisce*?" I'd laid down the law and wasn't about to budge from my declaration.

"I'll take Heaven to the meditation room and give her the broad strokes. Is that acceptable?" Maya asked.

"Hey, what about us? If Heaven gets the full story, why don't we?" Brenda asked.

"You don't want to test my patience, Brenda. Heaven we need, you, not so much. We took you on as a favor to Star." Leah glared at Maya. "See what you started? Are you happy now?"

Both Brenda and Maya seemed to shrink under Leah's sharp rebuke. When I glanced over at Francine, I thought she was about to hurl on the table, she looked so uncomfortable.

Leah was a bully, and she was making all of the women uncomfortable. I wasn't sure what was the right balance between assertive and confident, or aggressive and overbearing. Normally, I tended to hover around the meek and wimpy end of the continuum. I don't know why I felt the need to come to Maya's defense, but for whatever reason, I had developed a tiny backbone and decided Maya needed my bravery. "Leave her alone. You're as much a bully as those asshat government agents."

Leah opened her mouth, then quickly shut it.

Maya seemed to straighten her body. "Come on, Heaven. Let me show you the meditation room. It really is a special place, and I think we all need a little breather right about now."

I admired her ability to not respond to her sister. Maya had a quiet command and a gentler touch that I thought was a more effective way to handle the eccentrics from the Dream Center.

When she took my hand to lead me into another part of the house, I settled and left Leah and the other women gaping at us.

†

There was a frickin' tree growing in the middle of the meditation room, complete with babbling brook. The koi pond was stocked, and water lilies floated on top. I'd never seen anything quite like it in my whole life. There was some serious money in this house, and I wanted to know its origins. I grew increasingly uncomfortable. In my limited experience, money tended to corrupt people, good people. I didn't want Maya to fall into that category.

Maya led me to a stone bench set strategically in front of the koi pond. "What do you want to know?" she asked.

"Where did all the money come from?" I blurted out.

"Our father was an instrumental person in the Dream Center. He's made more money than anyone could possibly spend in a lifetime. This house was a mere drop in the bucket to him—a loss not nearly as painful as his prodigal daughters."

"I don't understand." I turned my head to look Maya in the eyes. The pain was evident in her expression.

"We were a means to an end. Our gifts did not come naturally. Father had the luxury of pumping experimental drugs into our system from the moment of birth until early adulthood. He didn't anticipate Leah's skill. She despises Father and has made it her life mission to destroy him and his work. He underestimated her talent." Maya shrugged.

"What about your skill?" I asked.

"I can hold my own, but I don't harbor as much contempt as Leah, nor do I seek to control things as much as she does. It's not in my nature. Our motives are at opposite ends of the spectrum. I seek to repair and help others become whole, as well as defend their rights to be free. She seeks to destroy everyone associated with the Dream Center, using her own private army of Weavers and Catchers. So far, she's not found enough talent to overcome my father's multiple layers of protection."

"You're using me." I didn't intend the statement as an attack, but I saw Maya flinch.

"Leah was going to get her way, no matter what objections I tossed in her direction. At least by accompanying you to our training center, I could try to make it less distasteful."

"So, what is the end game?" I asked.

"To shut down the Dream Center and destroy our father."

"Define destroy."

"Unfortunately, I don't know the extent of her plans for our father."

"What about your mother? Where is she in all of the maneuvering?"

Maya turned away from me. "I think I've given you sufficient information to satisfy your demands. It's time to continue your training."

I'd hit a sore spot. It wasn't hard to feel her reluctance to say anything else. I wasn't opposed to shutting down the Dream Center, but I wasn't sure how comfortable I felt about whatever collateral damage Leah hoped would occur.

"I'm only doing this, because for whatever crazy-assed reason, I trust you. Please don't let me do anything that I'll regret. I won't be a party to anyone's deliberate demise. I don't want that hanging over my head. It's one thing to shut down the center and quite another to cause someone's death."

"I'll do my best not to let it come to that. I don't particularly like or respect my father, but I don't want him dead either."

I grabbed Maya's hand, squeezed once, and nodded for her to continue. She led me to a very comfortable-looking day bed and gestured for me to lie down.

"Um…I uh don't really want to be psychoanalyzed or anything."

Maya chuckled. "I'm not going to violate your mind." She gestured toward the bed again. "I know this seems counterintuitive, but I want you to conjure up the biggest, scariest, apparition you can."

"I don't think that's a good idea, besides, I'm not a monster factory. I can usually only dream up something like that when I'm at a low point. No offense, but I'm not about to go down that dark path voluntarily for anyone, not even you."

"Heaven," she began patiently, "you won't be able to control your dream creatures, unless you can also control their birth. If you'd rather conjure up a protector of some sort, that'll work as well. Lie down and take deep breaths. I hate to do this to you, but I want you to imagine yourself entering a very dark tunnel. You're afraid. You're not able to see more than a foot in front of you, and that prickle of apprehension you feel before something awful is about to happen just crawled up your backside and burrowed into your skin."

I shivered, as I started to almost taste my fear. It was all around me, threatening to envelope me into nothingness. I hated this feeling. It never led to anything good. "Okay I'm there." My voice echoed in the room, almost as if the vibrations were bouncing off that dark tunnel.

"You need a protector, something that can help you fight the darkness. Bring your vision to life, Heaven," Maya urged.

She-Hulk was walking beside me, but she wasn't green like in the comic books; she was blue. I guess, since she was my apparition, I could make her any color I wanted, and any size. My protector was twice the size of the original She-Hulk, who I'd always thought was rather puny next to the Hulk.

"Nice," Maya said.

My eyes popped open and there she was. Like a superhuman, sexy, and really big Smurf. She crossed her massive, muscled arms across her chest and tilted her head.

"Epic," I cried out. "Can I keep her?"

Maya laughed. "No, Heaven, but you can conjure her up again in the future, if you wish."

I could feel my bottom lip protrude in a pout. "All right. What do I do to put her back in my head?"

"Well, you could either add to your action-figure collection or practice a mantra of sending her back. The mantra requires complete concentration. We don't want her to end up roaming the streets."

"Yeah, I know, that's kinda happened before," I said sheepishly. "Thankfully, they didn't stay long. Half an hour, tops."

"Later, we can practice keeping what you create, fully together and functioning for longer than thirty minutes. For now, you need to concentrate on sending her back to that place in your imagination where she originated. Imagine there is a place in your brain, where if you focus hard enough, She-Hulk will evaporate, almost like a genie. She'll simply swirl into that special place."

Her description made me think of a lazy tornado—like a combination of cigarette smoke and a whirling dervish in slow motion. As soon as that thought took hold, my She-

Hulk began to turn into a vapor-like substance, until poof, she was gone.

Maya smiled. "You are a very quick learner."

I was so damned proud of myself at that moment. All my life, I'd considered myself a fuck-up of immense proportions. I was at the very top of a pitiful mountain. For once, I was able to accomplish something without it going sideways. I felt good and didn't want to jinx anything.

"Can we stop now while I'm on a roll?"

"Yes, we can. You deserve a break. I think this calls for a sweet treat, since we both missed dessert. Chocolate chip cookies cure about anything that duct tape doesn't."

I scrunched up my face in confusion. I wondered if she thought something needed curing. Maybe I wasn't so successful after all. I didn't understand. All the air whooshed right out of my happiness balloon. "I thought I did well?"

"You did. I'm the one who needs…never mind. Let's just raid the cookie jar, okay?"

I'd never met a chocolate chip cookie I didn't like, so I nodded and followed her to the enormous kitchen.

†

I could smell the cookies well before we reached the kitchen. I wondered how Maya knew there would be warm, freshly baked treats waiting for us to pounce on them before they'd fully cooled.

Francine was bent in front of an open oven, pulling out a cookie sheet loaded with enormous chocolate chip cookies. I could almost feel the drool slip from my lips.

Maya grinned and whispered, "Francine hates conflict. Whenever she's stressed, she bakes and we benefit from her nervous energy."

I winced. "Did I cause that?"

Maya waved her hand in the air. "No, of course not. Leah was the one that caused this."

Francine must have heard us whispering. She set the hot baking pan on the black granite counter and pushed the oven door closed, then seemed to shrink back against the cabinets next to the stove.

Brenda, Star, Jimena, Deidre, and Raven all strolled into the kitchen. Leah was conspicuously absent, and I wondered if she was pissed about the earlier minispat. I almost started laughing, because they looked a little like one of those conga lines that usually start at a party after everyone has had several drinks. They were close enough to have put their hands on the hips in front of them, but they weren't kicking their feet to a snappy tune.

"Um…I baked cookies for everyone," Francine stated.

"Well, if it isn't Captain Obvious. I think everyone can see that you baked more cookies. We're all gonna be 500 pounds before we finish our training," Brenda snipped.

"Shut up, Brenda. Why do you have to be such a bitch? You must not be getting any. I don't blame Star for locking you out," Deidre snipped back.

"Mind your own fucking business, Deidre." Brenda took a step and got into Deidre's face. "You're just pissed, because I never offered to take you down pleasure lane. I do have my standards."

Maya gently pushed Brenda and Deidre apart. "Come on, guys, we have a common enemy, and it isn't each other. Personally, I love your cookies, Francine. Thank you for baking them. If you don't want to eat any, Brenda, then don't."

Maya grabbed the top cookie from the pyramid stack balanced on the plate. She took a big bite. "Mmmmm, delicious…orgasmic…it's all warm and gooey."

Brenda snatched the next cookie on the top. "I suppose I can find a good way to work it off." She winked at Star, then shot a lascivious grin in my direction.

I wasn't about to get involved in Brenda's petty games or respond to her mild flirtation, so I ignored her and grabbed my own warm treat. I had to agree with Maya's description. After I'd taken my first bite, I quickly grabbed two more. It looked like there were plenty for the taking.

"Is there any milk?" I mumbled, as I continued to chew.

Deidre pulled open the massive, stainless steel refrigerator and grabbed a carton of milk from the top shelf. Maya grabbed two glasses from one of the cabinets. "Anyone else want some milk?" She proceeded to serve up what I consider the perfect beverage to pair with cookies. The rest of the women shook their heads, and I wondered why they were passing this up.

"Thanks," I mumbled around my third bite. I picked up the full glass and gulped down the cold, creamy drink. "Ahhhh, that hit the spot. Can I take this to my room now? I'm kinda sapped."

"Me too, I'll walk with you." Maya grabbed a second cookie and her glass of milk, and followed me when I left the kitchen. When we got back to my room, she taught me one more nifty trick on how to control an apparition, before tucking me in and placing a kiss on my forehead. Apparently, I could envision all sorts of restraints for my monsters, including chains, locked boxes, a jail cell. The sky was the limit and only bound by what my vast imagination might summon.

CHAPTER TWELVE

I woke up from a deep sleep a couple of hours after I'd turned in for the night. My stomach felt a little sour. For a minute, I thought maybe the three cookies and tall glass of milk I'd had right before bed were the culprits, but I later discovered there was an entirely different reason for my discomfort.

I pushed down the covers and rolled out of bed. It was a little after midnight, and I didn't want to wake anyone else in the house. I began my foraging trip to the kitchen by quietly sneaking down the corridor. I thought, perhaps, a soothing tea would help to settle me.

As I got closer to the kitchen, the uneasy feeling began to rise, then I heard the voices in the library. I skidded to a stop and closed my eyes.

I don't know if it was instinct or a product of my brief training with Maya, but I imagined I was invisible, and a steel door separated my thoughts and feelings from anyone who wanted entry. The unease continued to grow, as Maya's voice gained clarity. It almost sounded like a radio dial was turned just enough that the signal was now crystal clear. The voices had abruptly stopped for a moment or two, before I imagined my invisibility, but now it was as if I was in the room with Maya and Leah.

"I don't care if Father is getting more desperate. You can't use Heaven like that. She didn't sign up for what you have in mind. I won't be a party to that."

"You need to separate your feelings and look at this logically. None of us are safe with Father's followers crawling all over the sanctity of our training center. You've not been the one to keep them out. I can't do everything. Every time I have to use my resources to hold them at a distance, I have less to train our army," Leah said.

"Army? Listen to yourself. You are buying into the same thing as Father. We're not at war. Destruction of souls is not the answer. We need to rescue the women he targets and teach them to defend themselves, not strike out in the same manner as he hopes to use them."

"Don't be so naïve, Maya. We *are* at war, and I intend to win. Shhh. I feel something. Someone's trying to penetrate our fortress again. Fuck. You need to get Heaven ready, and soon, or none of us are safe."

"Why don't you just do what you've done before and bring them to our side? Don't destroy another innocent. It isn't their fault they're being manipulated."

"Says the person who gave that guy the runs for two days."

"I didn't kill him."

"I bet he wished he was dead."

"Not the same, and you know it."

I could feel my energy draining and the steel door slipping, so I hurried back to my room and slipped under my covers before relaxing the barrier I'd thrown up. I wanted to listen to more of the conversation, since I was clearly at the center of it, but I knew the risk was too great.

After I'd pulled the covers to my chin, I heard my door squeak open. I kept my eyes shut.

"I know you're not sleeping, Heaven. The question is, how much of the conversation did you hear?" Maya asked. "If you wanted to keep your eavesdropping a secret, you needed to keep whatever barrier you used all the way up until you slithered under the covers again. I can teach you how to sustain the wall, but you need to trust me."

I was pissed. Every time I turned around, it seemed like Maya was violating that trust. I popped up and exploded all over her. "You want me to trust you, then stop having clandestine meetings and talking about me like I'm some disposable asset. You're no better than the assholes at the Dream Center. At least they weren't hiding their purpose for keeping me locked up."

Maya sighed. She walked over and sat on the end of my bed. "I'm doing the best I can. I don't want you involved in Leah's own private assault against Father and the Dream Center any more than you do, but she is right about one thing. They won't stop until they have you back under their thumb, doing God knows what."

I didn't get a chance to respond before a siren blared in the room, and blue and red lights began flashing above me. It looked like the top of a police car had descended from the ceiling. As I looked up, I wondered how in the world I'd missed that. "What the fuck? Where did that come from?"

"Get dressed. Someone has penetrated the perimeter. The alarm is usually in a hidden ceiling panel, unless something trips it. I've got a bad feeling. I'm picking up some very nasty vibes."

†

I scrambled out of bed and threw on my jeans and a sweatshirt. When I reached the hallway, it was pandemonium. My fellow trainees were in various stages of duress. Francine was the worst, as she huddled against the wall, rocking, with her hands over her ears. Deidre was trying to comfort her, but it didn't look like it was working.

Jimena was wide-eyed and caused a bit of a stir with the chain attached to her collar dragging on the ground. Raven, in a full set of leathers, ran down the hall with Maya. I still couldn't match the granola hippie-dippy I'd first met with the leather-clad dom. Maya and Raven looked like they were about to do some major damage as they dashed outside. I wondered where Leah had gone. She was suspiciously absent while shit was splattering all over the place.

I suppose, I could have conjured up my She-Hulk, but I wasn't exactly sure who to send her after. I didn't know where Brenda and Star were. I doubted that, even if they were hot and heavy in their room, they wouldn't have heard the commotion.

Although not knowing what to do, I jolted myself into action and headed in the same direction that Raven and Maya had gone. That's when I saw Leah standing on the back patio looking toward the edge of her property. I glanced at the spot she seemed to focus on and saw Maya crumple to the ground.

"Nooooo," I yelled. I began to run in Maya's direction, but Leah grabbed me and held me back. I was starting to create a living protector, when I felt something tighten in my head. That something slowed me down, but ten seconds later, She-Hulk appeared.

"It's only a dart, Heaven. They aren't interested in terminating us, merely capturing our greatest talent. At least they didn't get you. Listen, there are too many of them, and we're overpowered for now. At this point, we can barely keep them from taking more. Let them take her, for now. I promise, we'll get her back," Leah said.

I couldn't understand how Leah was calmly able to watch, as a man picked Maya up and tossed her over his shoulder without a second thought. I saw a blur of men take a step forward, then seem to register my big, blue protector. A second or two later, they disappeared in the lush foliage that surrounded Leah's property.

"Are you nuts? We have to go after her. It's not too late. She-Hulk, go," I ordered.

My blue mass of muscles started running toward where we'd last seen Maya.

"They'll kill Maya if you send your pet. I suggest you make her disappear for now," Leah calmly said. "I'll help you. Just imagine her disappearing like an ember finally losing its orange glow and turning into a pile of gray dust."

I was so confused, I didn't know what to believe. There was something about Leah that I didn't trust, but I couldn't take a chance, could I?

"Do you really want to be the reason those bastards kill my sister? They will do it for spite and to prove that my father is in total control, regardless of our ability to steal away their latest talent acquisitions."

I didn't want to be responsible for that. I already felt guilty for my earlier out-of-control dreams and the scientist who had paid the ultimate price. I knew he was only doing what he was told, but he'd been in the way. My dark protector only saw a threat that needed elimination. I'd live with that shame for the rest of my life. After it happened, I'd gone into a deep depression, which just made things worse. Each night, I'd summon a new monster, scarier than the previous version. I was placed in solitary confinement, so my dark dreams would no longer wreak havoc on anyone else. Eventually, they found the right mixture of chemicals to control me, and Syl was assigned exclusively to protect psycho Heaven. Her conscience had led her to do the right thing.

I shook those dark thoughts free and concentrated on sending She-Hulk back to my subconscious. I was getting more and more comfortable with her as my sidekick. She wasn't hairy and didn't have razor-sharp claws, but I knew she could do the trick in a pinch.

When I opened my eyes, Leah was smiling. "Good job, Heaven. You should go back to your room and get some sleep. We have a big day tomorrow, planning our attack on the Dream Center."

"Did they get Raven too?" I asked.

"Oh, yeah, right. I should check on that. I saw her go down, but I didn't see them take her. She'll probably wake up with a hell of a headache, but she'll be fine."

I hadn't paid much attention to Jimena. When I heard a sniffle, I looked back over my shoulder and saw her swiping at her eyes.

"Oh, stop crying, Jimena. Come with me, we'll go pick up your mistress and put her to bed." Leah waved her hand in the air and started walking.

I assumed she wanted Jimena to follow. I needed to help, so I trudged along behind Jimena and her dragging chain. If anyone had been watching, they probably would have burst out laughing at such a strange scene.

We followed Leah into the veritable Garden of Eden, Northwest style. We found Raven in a face plant next to a bush. Leah seemed unconcerned, but Jimena started blubbering again.

"She's only sleeping, no need to get all emotional. They used tranquilizer darts. It's not their style to eliminate a potential asset, so can you please stop caterwauling? You're getting on my last nerve. Help me pick her up." Leah grabbed Raven's right arm and started pulling her up, while placing a hand behind her back to help lift her to a pseudo sitting position.

I scrambled to the other side and grabbed Raven's left arm. Dead weight was a lot heavier than I'd thought. Not that I'd ever lifted an unconscious woman before. "Wow, she doesn't look like she weighs that much."

"We're definitely feeding people too much here," Leah grumbled.

"Are you saying Raven is fat?" Jimena asked.

"Stop being so damned sensitive and give the waif on the other side a hand."

"Hey, I'm not that bad," I exclaimed.

"You could eat more, Raven on the other hand…" Leah let her words trail.

We managed to sort of carry and drag Raven to the back patio, and plopped her in one of the deck chairs. I was huffing and puffing by the time we took a rest, and I briefly considered conjuring up She-Hulk. She could lift Raven and put her to bed without breaking a sweat. I opened my mouth to speak.

"No, save She-Hulk for when we really need her," Leah pre-empted my idea.

"But it would be a piece of cake for her," I argued. I didn't even question Leah's ability to penetrate my thoughts, but the violation didn't make me very happy. I needed Maya to help me shut that door. I hadn't come close to mastering that skill. Maya. I was more worried about her than I was willing to admit. If I needed to save my psychic reserves to help Maya, then I could drag Raven's chunky ass all the way up the curving flight of stairs.

Deidre and Francine's pale faces loomed large on the other side of the sliding-glass doors. How in the hell had they survived the Dream Center? They seemed far too fragile for the fun and games I'd experienced. Right about now, we could certainly use their help. I motioned for them to come on out and join the party.

Deidre cautiously opened the glass door and poked her face out. "Is Raven…uh…okay?"

Leah waved her hand. "Yeah, she'll be fine, but we could use your muscle to get her inside."

After we managed to put Raven to bed, I reluctantly returned to my bedroom and lay awake for a very long time before exhaustion finally overtook me. I was on the precipice of a very dark mood, and that was a dangerous place for me.

CHAPTER THIRTEEN

I was startled awake by the familiar sounds of destruction. *Here we go again.* Crashing, snarling, growling, banging, and the high-pitched screams of terrified women.

Over the utter chaos, Leah's calm voice reverberated through the sounds of what I suspected was the complete annihilation of her beautiful residence. "Go get Heaven, right now."

I reluctantly tossed the covers over to greet whatever monster I'd dreamed up. By the clattering pandemonium, I knew it was a doozy. After cautiously opening the bedroom door, I peeked out.

"Holy shit!" I exclaimed.

The snarling, drooling, scaly toed, green giant was truly the most frightening thing I'd ever conjured. He, I assumed it was male, was at least twelve feet tall, and I swear his fangs were a minimum six inches long. Hey! He didn't have any hair. I'd never created a reptile before. A frightening version of Godzilla was crashing through the hallway, smashing its large claws against the walls, as he attempted to swipe one of my fellow Dream Weavers.

"Heaven, don't just stand there with your mouth gaping open. Send that creature back to a dark corner of your mind. We can use him later, so don't completely destroy him," Leah directed.

I shook myself out of my temporary inaction and concentrated on a bland room where I could send Godzilla to the corner like a naughty child on time out. It was a trick that Maya had taught me after our cookie run.

No one was more surprised than me, when the green giant disappeared with a dramatic pop. In my mind, I saw him placidly sitting in the corner, as if he were waiting for my instructions on what to do next.

After several minutes of calm, I looked up at Leah. She simply nodded once, then smiled.

"Nicely done, Heaven."

"Nicely done? Are you out of your fucking mind?" Raven exclaimed. "I don't give a shit how talented you think Heaven is, she is a goddamned menace."

Apparently, Raven was not suffering any aftereffects from last night's raid, other than a surly mood. Jimena was shaking, as she hid behind Raven. Deidre and Francine huddled together a few feet away. I hadn't noticed them enter the hallway and wondered what secret space they'd emerged from.

Leah shrugged. "She controlled him, what's the big deal?"

"Are you not registering the rash of destruction?" Raven waved her hand in a semi-circle and pointed to the enormous mess.

There were large holes in the walls, with nasty claw marks from floor to ceiling. I tiptoed farther into the hall that led to one of the sitting rooms, and registered how my big lizard had reduced every piece of furniture to kindling and tiny swatches of material. There were scratch marks everywhere.

I cringed when I turned around and registered Raven's angry expression. She'd followed me to the tranquil space where all of us had spent some time relaxing. It wasn't as glorious as the meditation room that Maya had taken me to, but it had been a nice area to contemplate thorny issues.

"Nobody was hurt." Leah appeared with her calm expression.

"Only because we were fast enough to barricade ourselves in the safe room, while you calmly asked one of us to fetch the freak. You know, Leah, I think you're more bat-shit crazy than Heaven, and that is nearly impossible," Raven spit out.

I'd had about enough of Raven's angry outbursts. It wasn't like I'd purposely dreamed up the apparition. I'd warned them what I was like when my mood was dark. Both Maya and Leah had insisted they could help me control the dreams and demanded I not take any medication while they were teaching me. It wasn't my fault.

"You're pissing me off, Raven. Maybe I'll dream up a special present, just for you. I should have left your bulky ass out in the bushes last night. You might be the boss of Jimena, but you're not the boss of me." I left her gaping at me and stalked off to take a shower. I wanted to get ready and step up the timeline for that discussion with Leah about how to get Maya back.

When I returned to my room, I realized that Brenda and Star were noticeably absent from both last night's invasion and this morning's unfortunate incident. That made me increasingly uncomfortable. Were they so involved in shagging each other, they didn't hear all the commotion?

†

Leah was relaxing in the meditation room, when I found her after snooping all over the complex in my search for the mysterious leader. She lifted her head and smiled at me.

"Come in Heaven. I've been expecting you."

"You should have given me an injection last night," I blurted out.

She shook her head. "You are gaining control at a rapid rate. We cannot afford to tamper with your talent in any way."

"But Lizardman could have killed someone. Didn't you ever consider that? Raven's a bitch, but she's right. My monsters can and have killed before. They are quite capable of immeasurable destruction, including the death of innocent people."

"Surely, you don't believe that the scientists who held you in that laboratory jail are innocent."

"Syl is. She got me out, and I've put her in the line of fire on more than one occasion."

Leah frowned. "Hmm, Syl is an interesting woman. The jury is still out on her usefulness."

"What's that supposed to mean?"

"You are naïve, Heaven. People are not nice. There is always an ulterior motive."

"What's yours?"

"Oh, I believe I've made no secret about my desire to destroy my father. It couldn't happen to a nicer guy, either. I may have my own personal reasons for this, but ultimately it is the right thing to do for people like you and me. Maya too. He's a much greater monster than anything you can conjure up, and it will take your skill combined with mine to prevail over evil."

"I don't care about your motives, I only care about Maya. I want to know what we're going to do to get her back."

"Good girl. We need your passion. Maya is in grave danger, but he won't kill her, he'll just make it so she wishes she were dead."

I sat on the bench in front of the tree and looked expectantly at Leah. "What do you need from me?"

"I need you to allow yourself to be captured and let them believe they have you. Once you're secure in one of their cages, I want you to unleash your immense power on them before they have a chance to control you through drugs."

"I can't just conjure up a monster on demand. What do you think I do, water my dreams and then voilà, insta-apparition like some Venus flytrap?"

"I have faith in you, and I will be by your side to assist. They are going to believe they've hit the trifecta when both of us offer ourselves up in exchange for Maya's release."

"What about the rest of the Weavers? Where do they come in on this brilliant plan of yours? By the way, where are Brenda and Star? They've been noticeably absent during all of this."

"They have their orders and have followed them to a tee. Don't worry about them."

Leah was being purposely evasive. I didn't care for that, but my need to rescue Maya won out.

"How are we going to go about getting captured and making it look like they've won? It's not like they haven't been following me around for ages. They could have picked me up any time, but they haven't. I've got to wonder why not."

"You were untrained before."

"So…"

"An untrained Dream Weaver is dangerous. Their Catchers were unsuccessful. They are counting on your guilt and new-found control."

"Their Catchers? I don't remember anyone trying to train me. Unless you're talking about that one Catcher that Spartan sent. How the hell do they know I have more control now?"

"Yes, I would suspect there is a lot you don't remember of your time there. Don't underestimate my father. He has spies everywhere. I imagine someone has kept them informed of your progress."

"Syl would never betray me." At least I hoped she wouldn't, but then I remembered the disaster with the previous Catcher and how Syl had encouraged me to give her a try. Syl had seemed sincere when we learned the Catcher had turned and was working for Spartan.

Leah raised her eyebrow. "Mmm hmm, the jury is still out on Syl. She may be our greatest ally or a vaporous traitor."

I couldn't get my head around Syl being a collaborator after she'd rescued me. I knew there were memories still hidden that I wouldn't allow free, because they were too painful, but I wanted to keep my recollection of Syl's defiance pure. I couldn't bear to think of her as the enemy. For now, I would ignore those thoughts.

"So, what do I need to do?" I asked.

"Let's take a walk, Heaven. It's such a nice day. It would be a shame to miss the beautiful sunshine, don't you think?"

I looked at her like she'd grown horns on her head. The abrupt change of topic had me in a tailspin. I felt that unwelcome tug in my head, but this time I couldn't quite bring up the barrier. I felt exhausted from everything that had occurred over the last two days. Almost as if I was watching myself in a movie and could not do a thing to change my circumstances. Leah looped her arm in mine and pulled me to a standing position. We walked into her garden as if we didn't have a care in the world. I felt like I was in a trance.

†

Leah was chattering away as if we were old friends enjoying a casual stroll through her exquisite back yard. I put one foot in front of another, barely understanding what was happening. I remained mute in my dream state, as she pointed out the various plants and their medicinal properties. Although the morning air was crisp and the bright sunshine crystal clear, I felt like I was in one of those allergy medicine commercials where everything was hazy. She seemed particularly proud of the variety of flora that grew on her property.

"Lavender is a personal favorite of mine and grows quite nicely here in the Northwest. We use the plant to create a calming tea. There's a creamery, close by, that makes lavender ice cream. It's quite delicious. Would you like to try some?"

I mutely nodded. It felt like an alien had overtaken my body. I caught movement in the bushes to my right and turned my head. I opened my mouth to greet two of my fellow Dream Weavers, but before I was able to get the words out, I felt a prick on my neck. At first, I thought a wasp had stung me, but that wasn't at all what had happened.

CHAPTER FOURTEEN

I heard muffled voices and instinctively kept my eyes closed while controlling my breathing. For whatever reason, I believed I needed to convince whomever was talking that I was still asleep. The fuzziness started to fade, and I concentrated on listening to the conversation that was nearly out of reach.

"I hear you have a new device that will allow us to make use of the more powerful Weavers without needing the Catchers' help to control them," a deep voice said.

"General Carlson, it's still in the testing phase. I can't guarantee the results." *Spartan.* That voice was definitely Dr. Spartan, the lead scientist for the Dream Center.

Ah, the general was here, that made sense. I remembered how Carlson had paid the Dream Center an unannounced visit that happened to coincide with one of my more terrifying monsters. I'd overheard him say something about fighting for the funding each time there was a debate in Congress about military spending. Those vast military investments were supposed to pay for what I could conjure.

"I've informed the general about our plans for Heaven. She is the key to the other developments in our program, since you are still testing this monstrosity." I was willing to bet my last dollar this was the voice of the infamous Turnbull, who I'd figured out was Maya and Leah's nasty father.

"We've been keeping close tabs on her. Unfortunately, our intel informs us that your daughters have interjected themselves into the equation," Spartan answered.

"I'm well aware of my offsprings' involvement. Both Maya and Leah are exactly Heaven's type."

Bingo. Turnbull was in the room.

"There's also another fringe group involved. We aren't exactly sure who is leading them, but they're somehow connected to your daughters," Dr. Spartan added.

"I know about that as well. No thanks to any updates from you." I heard the sneer in Turnbull's voice. "All of these developments will work nicely into our plans."

I didn't need to see what was going on to hear when Turnbull turned his attention to the general. "The women work best in pairs. Although Heaven is powerful on her own, as a dominant Dream Weaver, one of my daughters may help her develop her underlying Catcher skills."

"Need I remind you of when we sent the other Catcher? Heaven did not connect with her at all. What makes you think this time will be different?" Spartan challenged.

"Because this time, it will involve one of my offspring. They are both very difficult to dismiss," Turnbull answered haughtily.

"Your daughter Leah despises you and Maya…" Spartan's voice trailed off.

"Just stick to the science of developing and enhancing the dream pairs," Turnbull spit out.

"How exactly does that work?" General Carlson asked.

"We discovered that when they develop sexual relationships and strong feelings of…'love' with one another, their skills are enhanced." I could hear the disgust in Spartan's voice.

"I don't care who these soldiers are sleeping with, as long as they get results. We don't have time to introduce morality into the equation. If we don't see results within the next six months, you won't like the government's response to your failure."

I found this twist fascinating. So, the government was now threatening Turnbull and Spartan. Maybe this would all blow up in their faces after all, but that didn't mean we wouldn't be collateral damage.

"Based on who Heaven was involved with before, I have no doubt that either Maya or Leah will catch her eye. All we have to do is let nature take its course before capturing them again," Turnbull assured. "It was a major setback when Rosie died." Bastard! I wanted to open my eyes and unleash my most terrifying creature on all of them for even uttering Rosie's name.

"Don't let your personal feelings on lesbians get in the way, Spartan. We need this program to progress while we finally have a sympathetic president in the White House. We had eight years of a president who wasn't in favor of enhanced warfare. I'm glad that woman didn't win, or we would have suffered through several more years of a president who tied our hands. Get these women fully functioning, Spartan, or you won't see the light of day. We'll find a way to shove you into a secret prison where no one will ever find you. That's what we do to traitors."

"General, please let me have a word with Dr. Spartan, then I'll walk you out. You can wait in my office."

I heard a door click open then shut. I kept my breathing even.

"Why is she still asleep?"

"I don't know, I told them to use a low dose. She should be waking soon."

"Is she able to control her weapons now?"

"I've been assured that her time with the Catchers was quite successful."

"At least that is one hurdle we don't have to jump. Now, in answer to her stubborn refusal to assist—Maya is the one to use, not Leah?" Turnbull's voice inflected a question into his words.

"So I've heard. We intend to use Maya as the leverage needed to make Heaven comply."

"She resisted our extreme measures when she stayed with us before. Perhaps she'll be less likely to tolerate those same tactics when used on someone she cares for. It almost worked for us before, then Rosie had to ruin everything. Let me know when she comes to." Turnbull sighed. "I don't want to permanently harm Maya, but she is expendable. Heaven, on the other hand, is not. We nearly caused permanent damage with our last round of incentives. It's a good thing Syl took her away. Those idiot handlers let their emotion get in the way of progress."

"She was ten times more stubborn than the others."

"I hold you personally responsible for that debacle. Don't make me regret my decision to retain you as lead scientist. You should have recognized her value when she resisted. Imbeciles. I work with a bunch of shortsighted amateurs. Is the new drug ready?"

"We are testing it on Maya. It appears to have promising results."

"I do wonder sometimes if I have underestimated my youngest daughter. That old parlor trick with the diarrhea was executed perfectly. I don't understand why General Carlson was not impressed, it can be quite effective on the battlefield."

"I don't think that was exactly what General Carlson had in mind when he advocated for funding of the program. We've been losing badly to the insurgents who are comfortable in their local terrain, regardless of whether it's in a harsh desert or dangerous jungle. The remote parts of the world are nearly impossible to defend against guerilla warfare. This Dream Center is Carlson's multi-billion-dollar answer, and I think it's time to pay the piper."

"Are you telling me how to run the center?" I could hear the quiet anger in Turnbull's voice. "You do know that pairs produce a challenge when one partner is killed. The other is worse than useless, that solo soldier becomes a liability. Control is no longer possible when that happens. You assured me this new machine and the drugs are the answer. Like the General said, I don't give a fuck about your personal feelings on the couplings between women. Heaven and Maya are key to the success of the program. This new drug had better work on Heaven."

"It will. The same principles apply equally to Catchers and Weavers."

"Good. Good. Perhaps the combination of the new drug and enhanced manipulation techniques will work in our favor. If not, let her see what is in store for Maya if she does not cooperate. I'm done playing games."

"We are still testing the new machine, as I said. At this point it is too unpredictable to use on Maya or Heaven."

"Fine, I'd rather you take a chance on other subjects. You can even use Leah if you think it will speed up the process."

It took all of my willpower to remain immobile. I could almost see Turnbull. I remembered his nervous habit of pulling on the hairs of his neatly groomed mustache, even though it was almost too short to grab a hold of. Finally, I heard a door click again. At first, I thought it was safe to open my eyes, then I heard Dr. Spartan mutter, "He is one cold son of a bitch."

I could feel him hovering over me.

I felt his cold hand touch my wrist.

"Hmmm, your pulse appears quite active for one who is peacefully slumbering. You might as well open your eyes, Heaven. I know you're awake. You probably heard our conversation. Well good, because you should know what's in store for you this time. We will achieve our goals, or Maya will suffer. You do remember our little sessions, don't you?"

I relented and stared into his cold beady eyes that I did remember all too well. Dr. Spartan, was a short, balding man with a large, hook nose. He reminded me of an overweight hawk. He'd always looked at me with a ghastly combination of lust and loathing. It was like he couldn't make up his mind which would prevail.

I had heard him muttering once, when he thought I was unconscious during one of our little training sessions. "Heaven is a flawless creature. Her long blond hair falling in waves against her back. Those eyes, with a color I can't quite pinpoint, deep blue sometimes, almost purple at others. She is unsettling and mesmerizing all at once. How can a vile lesbian have that wholesome, girl-next-door look with just enough sensuality to make her tantalizing? Full lips in a subtle shade of red, and rosy cheeks telegraphing youth and vitality. I despise her and desire her at the same time. If only there were a drug to make her beauty within my reach. Pray the gay out is not a reliable tactic."

I looked around. Not a lot had changed from my earlier stay at the center. The walls were that same bright white that almost hurt a person's eyes. I looked down and saw my wrists secured to the metal on the sides of the bed. The tinted window was on my left, and I was sure there were others watching our interaction. Who those others were, I didn't know. The machine that had caused numerous nightmares was innocently immobile to my right, and I shuddered when I saw it. The probes originating from the monstrosity snaked out and attached to various parts of my body like a gruesome octopus with its arms suctioned onto a chosen prey.

"I guess you didn't have enough money to redecorate. It looks exactly the same. That is a shame. I always thought a little color would improve the ambiance."

Dr. Spartan scratched his head. "I see that freedom has not improved your disposition. Your smart mouth is what got you in trouble with the handlers before. Mr. Turnbull might have warned me about doing irreparable damage to your mind, but there is a lot we can do to your body. You'll start begging well before we've exhausted every tool at our disposal." He smiled. "We have brand new techniques. We'll warm you up in preparation for the final act."

"Bring it on. I've learned a few things on the outside, and you won't like my personal development."

"You know, Heaven, you should be honored. The Dream Center carefully selects participants. We've learned that the more unhinged the subject, the more susceptible they are to my special serum. Since you know how valuable you are, you must be completely unstable. You need us to help you hone that skill. Usually, young girls with bipolar disorder are the most receptive and easiest to control when paired with a Catcher, but not you. You had to be different."

Dr. Spartan pushed a button on the machine, and I felt a jolt that managed to hit nearly every nerve in my body. The sharpness of the pain was something that was difficult to describe. It felt like fire penetrating deep inside.

"That's level one. We have nine more levels that only affect the body. Shall we bring in Maya, so you can personally witness how well she tolerates level three? That's as far as we've gotten."

I gritted my teeth, but couldn't control the moan that escaped.

He continued, as if the pain that I'd allowed him to see didn't matter or register with him. "You know it's such a pity how hard it was to work with the sociopaths. Even though their dream apparitions can be truly terrifying with the drugs used to enhance them, we've had such a devil controlling them, and the Catchers don't seem to have any impact. Even the gifted children with enhanced mind manipulation skills don't possess the necessary aptitude to get the job done. Now, those same Catchers paired with a freak like you... Well, you make an unstoppable team. The damn Catchers are hard to control as well, especially the ones like Maya or Rosie, whose acute sense of right and wrong gets in the way."

"Fuck you. Is there a reason you're taking me down memory lane or bothering to explain your bat-shit crazy theories?"

"I've been perfecting the skills of our subjects through a carefully constructed regimen of drug and behavioral therapy. In the past, there were times when the levels were not modulated enough, and we lost a few. They were expensive assets that we couldn't afford to lose. Turnbull was livid after we lost Rosie. I bet you didn't know that. But like I said before, we've learned to only affect the body, not the mind. Of course, we'll stop short of permanent damage."

I slammed my eyes shut. I was done listening to his craziness. I concentrated on envisioning She-Hulk smacking Dr. Spartan in his smug mouth. I didn't think it would work, but when I opened my eyes, there was my beautiful blue woman tossing him against the wall like he was a rag doll.

"My restraints. Hurry," I called out.

She-Hulk grabbed the restraints and pulled. My wrists snapped loose, and I hopped from the bed. Three large men rushed into the room and tried to stick a hypodermic into She-Hulk. I relished the roar that came from her mouth, as she swatted at the men like they were merely pesky insects.

As I ran out of the room with She-Hulk on my heels, flashing lights and alarm bells screamed in my ears. Bedlam always seemed to follow wherever I went. The hallways were like a complicated maze, and I had no idea where I was running from or to. I wanted to find Maya, but I didn't have the foggiest idea where to look. I flung open each new door, only to find the vacant eyes of other women I assumed were low-level Weavers and Catchers. I thought it was strange that none of the doors I tried were locked, until I came to the second to last one on the end.

When I tried to turn the knob, I felt the resistance and kicked the door in frustration. I moved to the one-way window and looked inside. Maya and Leah lay vulnerable and immobile on side-by-side beds, with their wrists attached to the bedrails in the same manner that I had experienced earlier.

She-Hulk smashed her shoulder against the door. Although it dented, we remained locked out. I felt stymied by a fucking barrier that I couldn't believe She-Hulk was unable to penetrate. She smashed against the door again, and it buckled a bit more. I was encouraged by the progress and thought that given a bit more time, we would be able to enter the room, but then what.

I heard the telltale crack, when She-Hulk crashed against the door a third time. Unfortunately, at the same time the crack registered, I felt that pesky sting again. Wasps were not generally found inside the sterile walls of my former residence. It was lights out again for me. My last thought, *Damn this is getting old.*

†

This time when I awakened, I was alone. It felt like they'd stuffed my mouth with cotton, and my head was killing me. The drugs must have had a huge impact on my ability to focus, because I couldn't concentrate on anything other than the notion that I was royally screwed. I hadn't managed to escape, and I was sure they had injected me with that new drug, which acted as a blockade on my ability to call upon one of my dream friends.

In my muted state, I didn't register when Dr. Spartan returned to the room. I assumed he was watching behind the one-way glass and waiting for me to shake off the effects of their latest round of drugs.

"Although that wasn't a very smart thing to do, Heaven, the upside is that it does confirm our intelligence gathering. You now have the ability to conjure up weapons in your fully conscious state versus the limitations of dreamland."

"Fuck you," I slurred the only words I managed to form in my fuzzy state.

"We'll let you become more clearheaded before we begin our work. Let me warn you that your little stunt caused the handlers to take out their frustration on Maya. We've advanced her training to level four. We have six more levels at our disposal. I could almost smell the burning flesh inside her body. It wasn't at all a pleasant aroma."

I closed my eyes again and let my sense of defeat blanket me into unconsciousness. I wasn't sure how much fight I had left, especially with the drugs blunting my edges and the only tool at my disposal severely dampened.

†

I felt the light shaking of my shoulders. My eyes popped open and the welcome view sent my heartbeat racing. *Maya*.

"We don't have much time. Leah is losing her hold," Maya whispered.

"Are you okay?" I almost didn't recognize my graveled voice.

"I'm fine."

She didn't look fine to me. There were dark circles under her eyes, and even though I didn't think it was possible, she seemed to have lost twenty pounds. I could see the pain in her eyes. Haggard-looking was an understatement.

I shook my head trying to remove the cobwebs. I know I was particularly slow sitting up, and Maya put her arm around my waist, helping me roll from the bed and begin to stumble toward the open door. The alarms sounded muted, but I could hear them blaring all around me. The flashing lights bothered my sensitive eyes.

We hobbled along the corridor. Raven, Jimena, and Leah looked like they were a thousand miles away at the end of the hall.

"Come on, come on, there are too many for Leah to control. We have to get out now," Raven yelled. "Can't our star Weaver conjure up something to help us out?"

"They used a new drug on her. That is no longer an option," Maya answered, as she began dragging me closer to our comrades.

"I told you this was gonna blow up in our faces," Raven said.

"Can we argue about this later?" Leah calmly asked.

My neck felt like rubber, bobbling all around, as I attempted to control my limbs so that Maya wouldn't have to do all the work. Finally, we reached the small group of warriors that would end up being my saviors. Raven positioned herself on the opposite side of Maya, and the two of them managed to basically carry me out the door.

The bright sunshine pierced my eyes, creating a sharp pain. When I closed them, I must have lost consciousness. The next time I opened my peepers, I came in contact with

Maya's concerned expression. I was spending far too much time on my back and not getting any pleasure for it.

CHAPTER FIFTEEN

Maya still looked like shit, but she was a very welcome sight to me. I was touched when I saw her eyes begin to water. She looked up at the ceiling.

"Oh, thank God, you're awake," Maya whispered.

"What happened?"

Maya frowned. "My sister did not carefully think through her half-baked plan."

"I don't understand."

"You and me both. Sometimes Leah is more like our father than I am comfortable with. She has a ruthless streak about her and accepts collateral damage as the price of winning."

I looked down and noticed that Maya was clasping my hand. When she saw where my eyes had traveled, she severed the connection.

"Why'd you do that?" I croaked.

"What?"

"Remove your hand."

Maya blushed. "Oh that. Um…I need to get the doc now."

"No doctors." I struggled to sit up, but Maya gently pushed me back down.

"Please, for me, will you let Syl check you out?"

"Syl?"

"Yeah, Leah called her after we managed to escape."

"I thought Leah doesn't trust Syl."

"She doesn't, but she trusts outsiders even less."

"What's your opinion?"

"Syl cares about you. That isn't a manufactured emotion. She also feels guilty about something. I'd like to think it is related to her role in detaining you, but we can't be sure about that."

"I don't want to mistrust Syl."

Maya nodded. "Can I get her now?"

"Okay, but don't let anyone else in."

"I won't. I promise. I'll not even let Leah come see you until you agree."

"Will you please fill me in on everything? Because I know there are major chunks that haven't been revealed. If Leah wants my cooperation, I need the whole story, not just bits and pieces."

"That's fair. I'll tell you everything I know. I don't care what my sister or anyone else thinks right now." Maya grabbed my hand, squeezed once, and exited the room.

I managed to sit up and look around. I was back in my temporary bedroom at Leah's house, and the warmth of the room was a welcome change from the white, institutional walls. I never realized how much peace the decorated room elicited. I focused on the painted forest that hung on the wall directly in front of me. The fall colors brought a smile to my face.

It felt like I'd just managed to push through the other side of recovering from the flu. My body felt like a truck had flattened me, and I was as weak as a kitten, but I was alive, and so was Maya.

The light from the hallway leaked into the room when Syl opened the bedroom door and entered. She smiled and shook her head. "I think I long for the times when you conjured up the voluptuous strippers. You are trouble with a capital T."

"I think whatever drug they gave me has definitely clipped my wings."

Syl frowned and walked to the bed. "Can you describe how you feel right now?"

"Like an elephant just sat on my chest and Leah burrowed in my head to remove any coherent thoughts."

Syl raised her eyebrow. "Interesting that you would mention Leah."

"I don't trust her, but the real question is, can I trust you?"

"Okay, I deserve that, I suppose."

"Can you just answer the question honestly?"

Syl sighed. "I may not have always made the right decisions, but Heaven, I am on your side."

I stared hard at Syl, hoping to detect any falsehood. She appeared sincere, so I went with my gut. "You were involved, right from the beginning, with Leah's plan, weren't you? That little show of opposition to working with a Dream Catcher was all for show, wasn't it?"

Syl shifted her eyes to the floor. "I'm sorry. I wasn't helping you control your gift. I needed help. Leah convinced me that she was the obvious choice. I should have listened to my gut and gone with another alternative. I don't know why I didn't. Perhaps Leah's gift penetrated my brain and led me in the direction she desired. I had no idea it would go so wrong. I still think it's dangerous to get involved with a Catcher. It plays right into their hands. Darla and I have been having a lively debate about this. They have the ability to turn both Weavers and Catchers with a new drug. I'm working on a neutralizer right now."

"All of you have to stop treating me like a fragile child. I can't be a part of the solution if I only know a tiny part of the plan."

"You've grown. I'm impressed. Can I run you through a few tests? I need to know how much their latest drug impacted you."

"Will they be dangerous to anyone?"

"No, I don't think they will. You have a lot more control than you used to, but I can't be one hundred percent positive until I run the tests. The new drugs were developed to blunt your control, because you were too dangerous unless they were able to obtain your cooperation. They were hoping to use Maya as leverage. Who knew you would fall in love with the Catcher."

"I'm not in love with Maya." I'd answered quickly, but the words didn't feel entirely true.

Syl ignored my retort. "The tests?"

I nodded.

†

I had no idea what level of exhaustion I could aspire to, but after Syl ran me through a battery of tests I had a pretty good notion. I felt like I'd walked to Antarctica and back—on my tiptoes. Fortunately, she informed me that whatever they had injected into my system had not caused irreparable damage. She'd even remarked that she could tell how much I'd learned under Maya's tutelage.

She'd found her answers and undoubtedly reported back to Leah that I was still valuable to her, but I hadn't learned a damned thing. She promised that they would fill me in when the time was right, but the priority was learning how the drugs had impacted my system, then allowing me to rest.

By now, a needle should have been my BFF, considering how many times I'd been injected, "for my own good," but I was a tiny bit leery when Syl wanted to take a blood sample. I agreed, because deep down I trusted her, almost as much as I seemed to trust Maya. Leah, not so much.

Syl damn near ordered me back to sleep and then left my room. Unnecessary, because sleep overtook me almost immediately after she went away. I was too exhausted to dream, and that was a good thing. I didn't want to have to rein in something that my subconscious decided to bring to life.

I can't say for sure how long I was asleep, and it didn't matter anyway. When I woke up, Maya was sitting in a recliner next to my bed. Her head was resting on her chest, and I thought she was fast asleep. When I stirred and pushed the covers down, she brought her head up and looked me in the eyes.

"How are you doing?" she asked.

"I'm okay, but if you have a new body to spare, I'll take it."

She laughed. "If I had a new body hanging in the closet, I would have already procured that for myself."

She looked a little less like total shit, but I could tell that she'd had a rough time of it.

"Tell me about what you remember from your childhood or formative teenage years?" she asked.

Well, that came out of the blue. "What? I'm not sure that talking about my childhood is very important right about now. I'd like some honest answers to a few questions."

"It's important, Heaven. There are a few holes in…"

"Are you saying you might not have all the answers to my questions?" I asked.

"I think that there are some things that Leah has kept from me. Maybe you and I can cut through some of the bullshit by pulling together remote pieces of the puzzle. It's important."

"Okay. Well if you want to know if I was always like this, the answer is no. I think I always feared that I'd be the one to inherit my issue. Adults don't realize how big little people's ears really are. I would hear them whisper about how it skipped a generation, and the odds weren't in my favor."

"So, when did you notice you had special talents?"

"Ha, I like that…special talents. My folks were always hovering over me and watching. I eavesdropped on them talking one night about a promising program that might keep me from turning out just like my grandparents. I was pretty much doomed, because both my maternal and paternal grandmother suffered from bipolar disorder. I think they believed they were doing the right thing by me."

"And this program," Maya prompted.

"My parents tried to tell me it was like a camp for special teens. Before all the white coats got ahold of me, I never conjured up monsters. I had some major ups and downs, but I wasn't a menace to society. They should have left well enough alone."

"You're not a menace, Heaven."

"Tell that to the scientist who got his throat ripped out and bled to death before they stuck a hypodermic needle in me and the big hairball slipped back into my head. I don't remember everything they did to me, but I'll never forget the injections." I shuddered. "I hate needles. They strapped me to a bed. They made me watch stuff."

"How old were you?"

"Almost fourteen. I was sullen and difficult to deal with, increasingly more so than when I'd tried to off myself and ended up in the emergency department. The folks were at their wits end and convinced themselves I needed a consistent regimen of treatments over a long span of time. The doctors at the Dream Center assured my parents that the results weren't instantaneous and would require years of therapy."

"Did you ever try to tell your parents what was happening?"

"Nah, I formed a bond with some of the other kids at the ranch. That's what I called it, the ranch. I had a huge crush on this girl, and I figured the price of getting to hang out with her and learn about love was worth it. When they weren't doing their little treatments, we did get to have fun."

"How long did you receive 'treatments?'"

"Four years, then they let us leave. I was eighteen, and Rosie and I decided we'd had enough. We never questioned why they let us leave. We just figured, since we were eighteen, we were considered emancipated adults. We were going to get jobs, find our own apartment, and try to make a go of it. We did okay, even started college part time but, things didn't work out…" I decided I didn't want to tell any more of my story. I wasn't sure how that would help fill in the holes, and I wasn't interested in tearing open that sore. It was painful enough the first time around.

Maya glanced at me sympathetically, and I figured she knew she'd hit a tender spot. I was deliberately keeping those memories from popping to the surface, and I got the sense that she was trying not to invade my personal memories. "I think my father's group actively sought out potential kids to experiment on. He was especially interested in kids with mental health issues, or at least the potential for the issue to show up later in life. The other group of kids he focused his energy on were highly intelligent teens. His arrogance regarding the assumed intelligence of his offspring determined our inclusion in the program almost from birth. We later tested above an IQ of 140 and that cemented his assumptions."

"You were at the Dream Center?"

Maya shook her head. "No, there are multiple locations in addition to the main lab where all his adult soldiers end up. You already know how much worse that place is than what you called the ranch. Are you hungry? I'm starved."

I suppose Maya had her own raw lesions to contend with, so I took her cue that it was time to stop the heavy conversation. Besides, I suspected that Leah was the one I ought to be pinning to the ground and forcing to confess.

"Yeah, I am, and I think I deserve another one of Leah's specially prepared meals. At least I get gourmet food while being locked up in this mansion."

Maya frowned. "Does it feel like you're jailed here?"

"Yeah, kinda. But like when I was at the 'ranch,' there's someone I want to hang with, so it's okay."

CHAPTER SIXTEEN

All the usual suspects sat around the formal dining room table, with the exception of Brenda and Star who were suspiciously absent, again. In their places were Darla and Syl. I didn't want to make any comparisons, but I briefly thought about the famous pictures where Jesus regally sits in the center, among his apostles at the Last Supper. Leah was sitting in the center with an uncharacteristically grim expression on her face. I'd never seen her be anything but calm and confident.

Maya touched my arm and led me to an empty seat next to Syl, then sat on the other side. She briefly caressed my thigh, but it wasn't sexual. It felt more reassuring than anything.

"Where are Brenda and Star?" I asked.

"They're still inside," Leah answered.

"You left them in that horrible place?" I glared at Leah. She was becoming a very unpopular person in my opinion.

"They are still more valuable to us inside." Leah poured herself a glass of wine. "I may have made a few errors in judgment over the last few days, but I think maintaining their current position inside is to our benefit. I plan on making some corrections. I've come to realize how much I underestimated my father. We'll finish this spectacular meal my private chef has prepared for us, then I'll fill everyone in on the new direction we need to take."

I tried to catch each person's eye to ascertain how the others felt about Leah's declaration. Even though she'd delivered the proclamation with her usual calm demeanor, I could detect the stress that hovered around her edges. Each time I looked at one of the women sitting at the table, they hastened to look down or away. No one was saying shit.

Maya leaned into me and whispered, "I promise you'll get answers to all your questions. I had a heart to heart with Leah, and she agreed it's time to approach this differently. I think she was finally shaken to the core regarding the lengths that our father will take to achieve his goals."

An attractive woman in a white chef's coat and hat pushed out a cart with the most beautiful array of sushi and sashimi I'd ever seen. My mouth watered. I didn't make a lot of money when I lived with Syl, so affording high quality sushi was nearly impossible. There were four large trays packed with the delicacies.

"Thank you, Hana. This looks exquisite."

After we all feasted on the sushi and sashimi, Hana brought out a tray of mochi. Soft, pounded, sticky rice cakes surrounded a variety of ice cream flavors. I know most people would probably turn up their noses at flavors like red bean or green tea, but I preferred those unusual options, which Hana had included as well. I selected the more exotic treats.

"Oh, my God, so delicious." I grabbed another red bean mochi and stuck it in my mouth savoring the burst of sweetness and cold as it melted on my tongue.

Maya winked at me, as she slowly rolled around the Japanese version of an ice cream treat in her mouth and moaned her delight at the choice of dessert.

I leaned back in my chair and placed my hands on my bulging stomach. I was beyond full. I probably shouldn't have picked up the last piece of mochi. It was my undoing.

Leah had a genuine smile on her face, when she looked in my direction. "Did you enjoy the meal?"

I nodded. "Yeah, but I probably overindulged."

Leah clapped her hands. "Everyone follow me to the meditation room, and we can talk about what went wrong and how we plan to correct the situation the next time we attack the center."

No one offered any resistance, so I pushed myself away from the table and followed the rest of the sheep. I was marginally settled when Maya made sure to sit close beside me. Besides, I wanted Leah to fill in the blanks. There were some serious bald spots that needed hair plugs.

†

Someone had brought several comfortable chairs into the room with plush cushions, and we sat in a semi-circle. I was thankful that Raven was strangely subdued. She hadn't hidden her displeasure with me the other day, but tonight I also detected grudging respect.

Leah placed her hands on her thighs and began, "I confess that the plan we had devised was a bit shortsighted."

"We?" Maya raised her eyebrow.

"Touché, little sister. I suppose I should not have operated in a vacuum."

"It might have been nice to know that my abduction was part of your not-so-brilliant plan to get Heaven engaged and fired up enough to bring out the big guns. Was that your plan or did someone else inspire the ill-conceived scheme?"

My mouth was probably hanging unattractively open at this moment. "You what? Maya's kidnapping was all a ruse? You could have gotten her killed," I growled.

"I didn't think my father would take things that far. What kind of person sacrifices their own daughters?"

"I heard your father speaking to Spartan, while I pretended to still be out cold. He had no qualms about doing just that and considering her death collateral damage." I felt ill at the prospect of following Leah's cold, calculated plans. She was almost as bad as her father, and it seemed like the two of them were cut from the same cloth. I looked at Syl. "Please tell me you weren't a part of this."

Syl looked away.

"How could you?" I choked out.

"I only made the arrangements for you to connect with Maya after Leah convinced me it was the right thing to do. I swear I didn't know about the rest," Syl defended. "I should have listened to Darla," she mumbled as an afterthought.

I wondered what that was about and decided I'd corner her later to find out.

"Nor did I," Maya added.

"Water under the bridge. No sense in rehashing our failures," Leah defended.

"Are you fucking kidding me?" I yelled.

"Look, you may not like my methods, but the first time you ever conjured up a decent protector was when Rosie was threatened. I thought this was the right tactic. We can't afford to fight among ourselves. My father is a real danger to all of us. Not to mention the danger to every single Weaver and Catcher he's created over the years. Some we aren't even aware exist out there. His network is vast."

I could feel my face lose color when she mentioned Rosie. That was not a memory I wanted to explore, at all. I catapulted from the chair and ran back to my room. I didn't have anywhere I considered my safe space, but my room was the only location I didn't believe was somehow tainted with treachery or deception.

†

I was holding my head in my hands in an attempt to push back the memories. Twice, I'd been forced to revisit my memories with Rosie, and I didn't want to go there again. Three times was definitely not a charm.

The soft knock on my bedroom door caused me to sit up and brush away the tears.

"Heaven, it's me," Maya softly called out. "Will you please let me in?"

I sat for a few seconds and pondered what I really wanted. *Do I want to let Maya in? Am I prepared to talk about Rosie?* I had to admit that when I was around Maya, she was my safe place. I slowly emerged from the bed where I was sitting.

After I opened the door, Maya gathered me in her arms. "I am so sorry, Heaven. I wish I could go back in time and do everything all over again. I never wanted to see you in pain," she said while stroking my back.

"How much do you know about Rosie?" I asked, after we separated from her comforting embrace.

She took my hand and led me back to the bed. When we sat, her hand was still clasped in my own.

"I know she was important to you. I don't have the intimate details of what occurred, but Leah gave me the broad strokes."

"Did she tell you it was all my fault what happened?"

"No, because I don't believe for one second that's the truth. It may be your perception, but that does not make it reality. If you want to talk about it, I'm a good listener."

We sat there for several minutes without talking. I appreciated that Maya did not feel the need to fill in the empty space. Silence isn't always comfortable for people, and in their discomfort, I've often found they have a compulsion to add comments or questions where none are required. I know that time is sometimes elusive, but I imagine we sat there for at least five minutes, Maya patiently awaited my response. I was sure she would accept whatever direction I was willing to go with the conversation.

The dam finally broke. "Rosie was my first love. Some would have labeled it puppy love and not something with enough depth to…" My voice quivered for a second. "Her loss was a pivotal moment in my life."

Maya didn't say a word, she squeezed my hand, and that was her only encouragement for me to continue.

"Rosie was a Catcher. I don't think they realized what a bond they created when they teamed us up. We were hard to handle as individuals, and when they paired us, we were double trouble. At the time, I didn't understand how things worked, exactly. Now, I have a better idea. Weavers and Catchers are meant to work together, aren't they? A successful pairing is what allows your father to exploit us, right?"

Maya nodded. "I think my father was hoping that you and Leah would become his star team. I was just the carrot or stick to get you both to do his bidding. My father has always judged Leah to be the more powerful one. Fortunately for us, as much as we underestimated my father, he underestimated both you and Leah."

"How do the Catcher and Weaver teams work?"

"Weavers create and Catchers help to control the creations. You are unique because you have a little of both at your disposal. That is what makes you so dangerous and so desirable to control. You, Heaven, are one of a kind."

I wanted to confess everything, so I continued with my story on Rosie. I needed to say the words out loud, because I sensed Maya had imposed restrictions on her skills and would not step over the line to gather the information without my permission. "We were doing fine on our own. Even though Rosie and I didn't have a lot of money, we were in love and happy in our small apartment. Rosie was the one who noticed the black car one day, and we knew they would never leave us alone."

"My sister may be many things, and ruthless is an understatement, but she's right about one thing. As long as my father is alive and controlling the institute, they will never leave us alone."

"A lot of people think that someone with bipolar disorder flips between their highs and lows more rapidly than we really do. After Rosie and I left the institute, I managed to stay on a high, or at least not fall into a pit. She was good for me. In those four years, I never conjured up a monster. Sometimes, what I did dream up did not make Rosie happy, but they were never dangerous."

Maya chuckled. "With your creativity, I'm sure some of them were quite funny."

"Not to Rosie. She had a small streak of jealousy and was none too amused when I would dream up voluptuous strippers or pole dancers. I thought she should be flattered, since they all resembled her. When Rosie and I were together, my creations would disappear in a manner of seconds. After Rosie, my little innovations would remain in the world of the living for at least thirty minutes, sometimes longer. Unless they injected me, then the apparitions would disappear in seconds."

"What happened to Rosie?" Maya prompted.

"I was never sure why they decided to nab us after four years of leaving us alone. One night, we were walking home from our weekly date night out. We would scrounge for change and pull together enough money to treat ourselves to pizza on Friday nights. We weren't paying attention to the car that was following us. It was dark, and we took a shortcut through the alley. That's when the men grabbed us." I started shaking as I relived the night.

Maya pulled closer and began stroking my hand. The repetitive motion relaxed me enough to continue.

"I think they had injected me with some kind of suppressing drug. When I woke up and saw Rosie strapped to the bed next to me, I struggled and tried to get my bindings off. I was screaming my head off, but Rosie didn't open her eyes. She was so pale. Even though she wasn't conscious, I saw pain etched across her face. Her body was jerking against her restraints, and I knew she was having a whopper of a nightmare, but I couldn't get to her." My voice rose in agitation, as it all came flooding back.

"Let me guess, Dr. Spartan paid you a visit."

I nodded. "He did. He told me he could make our lives a lot easier. All we had to do was work together and do our patriotic duty. He sounded disgusted. I guessed that whatever he had done to Rosie hadn't convinced her to cooperate. She looked so fragile. I told him, I'd do whatever he wanted if he let Rosie alone. I was rapidly spiraling into that dark hole, and I guess when he injected me again, he didn't realize how much my despair would result in the kind of monster no one wanted released into the world. After Rosie died, they never found a way to control me or my dreams. That's why they let Syl set me free, isn't it?"

"Heaven, I have a piece of the puzzle you might not know about. Rosie was more like you than me. She wasn't just a Catcher."

"But she never conjured up any monsters or strippers when we lived together. I don't understand."

"Her strength was as a Catcher. She could not only control your visions, but she controlled her own and never let you see what she was capable of."

"Why? Why didn't she trust me?"

"I don't know the answer to that, Heaven. I don't think we'll ever know, but I don't believe it was a matter of trust."

"When I woke to the chaos in the small room they had confined us to, there was a snarling fiend ten times more powerful and terrifying than anything I'd ever dreamed up in the past. He was tearing up the room, and when I looked over to Rosie she seemed resigned to her fate. One swipe of his claw, and the light in her eyes disintegrated. He'd disemboweled her. The oddest thing occurred after that…"

"He shrunk in size and became less menacing."

I looked at Maya, and my surprise at this revelation was probably evident. "How'd you know?"

"Heaven, the beast was not solely your creation. What came to life in that room was your combined energies. They'd tapped into both of your darkest thoughts, combined like a nuclear reaction. I can't know this for sure, but I think Rosie didn't want them to use you. She did the only thing she could. She took away their leverage."

"Suicide by apparition?"

"Yes. Remember when Leah said the second generation of Weavers and Catchers usually committed suicide? A few of the third generation did that as well," Maya whispered.

Maya pulled me up, turned down the covers and helped me crawl under the sheets. She joined me and wrapped her arms around my body, as I cried myself to sleep.

CHAPTER SEVENTEEN

I was surprised when I woke up and the room showed no evidence of a wave of destruction. I turned to look at Maya, and she smiled.

"Morning. We should shower, because I have something fun planned for today."

"What are you talking about?" I asked incredulously.

"Fun. We haven't had much in the last few days and that is a crying shame." Her perky morning voice was a jolt of energy, but I was still a bit hesitant to leave the comfort of my safe space.

"Um…have you forgotten about the bad guys that consider you are acceptable collateral damage? Are you out of your fucking mind?"

"Pish Posh. I refuse to live my life in fear. Besides, now that we know the score, we can become an unstoppable team.

I wasn't expecting to get nabbed from Leah's fortress, but when I'm out and about, I can easily detect reprehensible thoughts before they turn into action. I was also encouraged to see Darla here last night. That definitely increases our chance of success. Besides, you are much better at controlling your gift. Together, we'll strike back before they can say Howdy Doody."

Once again, I wondered how Darla factored into this whole mess, besides being Syl's girlfriend, but I pushed that out of my mind and answered, "You're nuts."

"Tick tock, Heaven. Time's a wasting. Life is a savory treat, meant to tickle our taste buds, not a bland trudge through a barren desert."

Why do I want to follow this woman wherever she goes? I had to finally admit I was smitten with her in the same way that Rosie had charmed me. Rosie had always been the instigator whenever we got in trouble. Her bright light was extinguished far too soon. I didn't want that to happen to Maya. I was putty in her hands.

"I'm not going to hold back any longer. Life is too short. Time to grab the bull by the horns. If you want to join me in the shower, that's all right by me." She pecked me on the lips and jumped from the bed.

I followed the female Pied Piper. My mouth went dry when she shed her clothes and turned the knob of the shower. The gentle spray of water from the upscale nozzle pushed out a thousand tiny droplets to create an erotic visual display. Maya leaned her head back and accepted the misty liquid on her face.

I yanked off the jeans and T-shirt that I'd slept in and walked into the tiled enclosure. I wanted to touch her silky skin and reached out to lay a tentative finger on her shoulder.

She must have sensed me, because she took a small step away from the spray and her eyes opened to look at me. She grinned and brushed her hand against my cheek.

"I won't break if you touch me, Heaven. I'm not made of glass, and I do so want to feel your hands on my body."

Holy shit, I thought, *I'm finally going to have sex.*

"Not sex, Heaven. I don't have sex, I make love."

I spread my hand out and let it travel slowly down her breasts. It had been so long since I'd been intimate with someone, I wasn't sure what to do, where to touch first.

"You're so beautiful," I said, then I noticed the angry, red mark on her flawless body. I frowned and was about to say something, when Maya interrupted my thoughts. I never got around to asking her about the mark.

Maya smiled. "It's like riding a bike, Heaven, riding a bike."

I'd never been a very confident person and was experiencing a fair amount of performance anxiety. Then I had this ridiculous image of a dancing bear performing for her master, and I worried that somehow, we'd soon be sharing the shower with a large, black bear in a tutu.

Maya gathered me in her arms and brought our mouths together. She explored every inch of my lips as she kissed me. She was gently sucking on my bottom lip, and I melted into the embrace. My hands began to work their way up and down her backside of their own volition.

"That's it," Maya encouraged. "Don't overthink things."

Sometimes, I was my own worst enemy. *If I decide to traverse her body and taste her, will it be difficult with the water cascading over us? If I slather soap over her, will I know if the slippery feeling is the soap or her arousal? Will I get a mouthful of suds if I decide to go down on her before she's thoroughly rinsed?*

Maya leaned her head back and roared with laughter.

Fuck. I was pretty sure I'd just ruined everything with my propensity to analyze every little detail. At least I hadn't conjured up the bear.

"Maybe our first time should be in a bed, Heaven. It appears as though the mechanics of the shower have you flummoxed."

"Um…uh…." I stammered.

"It's okay, but you're still washing my back, because that is the least I can expect of a shower partner." She turned around and slicked backed her hair away from her face, as she reached for the shampoo. After pressing on the pump twice to collect a palm full of lavender smelling soap, she began to rub it sensually into her scalp.

I scrambled to squirt a healthy amount of the citrus shower gel onto a pink mesh pouf. I used my hands to agitate the bath accessory until suds appeared, then began lightly scrubbing her back.

"Mmmm. That feels nice. I can't manage to scrub those hard to reach spots. Thank you, Heaven."

My eyes rolled up in my head. *Oh no, thank you.* My own feelings of arousal and joy overwhelmed every part of my body, as I snaked my hand down her hip and around to her stomach, while my other hand continued to wash her back with the pouf.

Baby steps. At least we were both naked together. I felt relief that I was spending some intimate time with Maya. For now, that was enough. For all my blustering about needing to have sex with someone, anyone, even one of my conjured strippers, I wasn't ready. Not yet.

†

I was both disappointed and relieved that we hadn't made the trip directly to the bed after the shower. Maya acted like nothing had gone awry with our little shower escapade. The coitus interruptus was completely ignored, as she dressed and hurried me along.

"Layer up, Heaven, because we're going to be outside all day long, and it will probably get warm. There's nothing like spending time in the fresh air and enjoying nature."

I thought we might go on a hike, and that was okay with me, but when she dragged me to a hall closet and removed a puffy, yellow life vest, I groaned. The water was nice to look at, but I didn't know how to swim and wasn't all that excited about going anywhere that required a person to wear a bulky flotation device.

"Um…I never learned how to swim. I have a sneaking suspicion that whatever you have planned, I won't enjoy."

"Nonsense. That's what the vest is for. You don't need to learn how to swim if you wear the life vest the whole time we're on the water. Besides, I am an expert lifeguard. You have nothing to worry about."

Her assurances for my safety didn't do a whole lot to settle my nerves, but I supposed if I was really evaluating the danger swirling all around me, a trip on the water was the least of my problems. The minute we climbed into her car, I felt it. Someone was tracking our every movement, and I felt their fear. Bits and pieces of their thoughts floated through my head. If they weren't able to track us and keep us in their line of vision at all times, the loss of their job was the least of their concerns.

I glanced at Maya after I clipped my seatbelt in place. She had a strange look on her face.

"Your power is increasing exponentially."

"Huh?"

She eased down the long driveway. When she pressed a button on the remote clipped to the sun visor, the large iron gate opened. She pointed to the black sedan idling on the side street outside the gate. "You knew they were there. How would you like to do a little test of your new powers?" She grinned widely.

I hesitated. "Um…okay. What did you have in mind?"

"Do you know how Catchers operate?"

"I have a general idea, but not exactly."

"I know you've felt Leah's unwelcome tentacles inside your head, and you are the only person who has ever been able to block her. Essentially, Catchers can teach control as well as direct a Weaver's creations. To varying degrees, we can also read thoughts and control a Weaver's emotions. Our gifts expand tenfold with everyone else."

"You mean *normal* people."

"No, I was referring to those without our special gifts."

"Okay, so what does that have to do with this test you want to perform?"

"Heaven, I believe that my father has continued his work. His desire to make Weavers and Catchers more potent centers around you. He knows you have both talents, and I think he injected you with something that would enable you to increase your potential when combined with a Catcher. Are you game?"

I nodded.

Maya screeched off, and I grabbed the "oh shit" handle, as she barreled down the road putting a considerable amount of distance between us and the car attempting to follow us. I don't know how she did it, but she managed to lose the car. It didn't make a lot of sense to me, but somehow, I knew they were over five miles away when Maya managed to pull over to the side of the road.

She turned her head and smiled at me. "Normally, we would not be able to either sense them or make any suggestions at this distance, but I believe, if we come together as one with a single directive, we can reach them. I think a sudden onset of the stomach flu will do the trick."

"You want me to imagine that the two dudes in the black car are suddenly overcome with extreme nausea."

"Yes, I want them to feel compelled to pull over and vomit nonstop for the next twenty minutes."

"That's kinda mean isn't it? I'd rather have pneumonia than the stomach flu."

"Heaven, if directed to do so, they would torture you or I without a second thought about ethics. So no, I don't think that is too cruel. One of them was directly responsible for…"

She left the words hang in the air, and I knew she'd been tortured. That was enough for me to toss my ethical dilemma aside. "Okay, what do you need me to do?"

Maya grabbed my hand. "Together we need to imagine that a nasty norovirus is burrowing into their bodies. Let me put a picture of the virus in your head, so you know what it looks like. It's actually kind of pretty, almost looks like a blue crystal."

I was shocked when the picture popped into my head. I thought it looked more like a blue sea anemone, but I didn't want to split hairs, because her ability to inject that picture into my mind was nothing short of spectacular. I had a fleeting thought that maybe Maya wasn't being completely honest with me, and that she was far more powerful than Leah but wasn't letting that secret out for anyone to exploit.

"Okay, I see it. Now what?"

"Now we push that tiny blue menace into their bodies and direct it to do its thing. We need to imagine that the effects are instantaneous. Are you ready?"

I nodded. I probably looked like I was constipated, as I slammed my eyes shut and concentrated on doing exactly what Maya had suggested. For a brief moment, a wave of nausea hit me, then went away.

I felt Maya's fingers brush my cheek, and I opened my eyes.

"Sorry, I forgot to warn you that you might feel the effect of our suggestion once it took hold."

"So, it worked?" I asked.

"Oh yes." The tinkling of her laughter filled the car, as she pulled out into the road and we headed for whatever body of water she decided to take us to. I'd had a major clue what fun we were about to embark on when I saw the sleek, fiberglass kayak attached to the roof of her SUV. I'd never been in a kayak before and it was slightly unnerving to me.

CHAPTER EIGHTEEN

I erroneously assumed we would drive to some nice, calm lake and paddle around on the smooth, glass surface. I would survive my first kayaking adventure without catastrophe. I was wrong.

On the way to Camano Island, which was where we ended up, the conversation was light. I suppose neither of us were prepared to talk about the shower-interruptus morning. That was what I'd affectionately called my stupid hesitancy to, as Maya put it, take the bull by the horns. I didn't want to know what I meant to Maya, because I was afraid I was a passing fancy for her, and that wasn't at all how I felt about Maya. I knew I would eventually broach the topic, but I was embarrassed and thought a few more hours wouldn't hurt anything.

I questioned my logic, as we pulled into the park and I realized we were about to launch the kayak into Saratoga Passage—fucking Puget Sound—not some calm lake. Sure, it was gorgeous. I could certainly admire the surroundings, as I looked out on the blue-green water bordered by lush green trees and foliage that grew so well as a result of the ample rain that fell on this part of the United States.

"Um…Maya. Have you forgotten that I don't know how to swim and have never kayaked even once in my life?"

"Hey, don't worry, the water's not that cold if we fall in." She opened the door and jumped out.

Maya was just plain crazy. The sound didn't ever get warmer than sixty degrees at the height of summer, and I knew, today, it would probably hover around fifty. I also knew that the depth of the passage was nearly 600 feet, which was 595 feet more than I was comfortable with.

"Are you trying to kill me?" I cautiously emerged from the safety of the SUV.

Maya's face scrunched up, as she started to remove the tie-downs that secured the vessel of death. "No, of course not. I want you to experience life, Heaven, and so far, you haven't done much of that. How do you know the kind of activities you'll enjoy, if you never venture outside your comfort zone?"

I suppose she had a point, but ziplining and kayaking were a bit too adventurous for me. "Why couldn't we do this on a nice, calm lake? Or maybe in a sturdy plastic kayak that isn't so prone to tipping over?" I began to help her remove the fasteners, despite my fear.

"Do you trust me, Heaven?"

I knew that she'd either kept things from me or purposely led me astray; so blind trust wasn't exactly something I could admit to, and yet, I did trust her on the big things. I considered keeping me safe a very big thing. "I trust you to keep me safe," I said honestly.

She frowned. "That's fair. I haven't always given you all the information you need to be prepared for the challenges that will continue to cross our path until my father is neutralized. I need to fix that. Soon. Can you help me lift the kayak?"

If I was going to drown in Saratoga Passage, I figured I deserved to know the answer to the question I'd been dying to ask. I took the conversational risk, that would be my bull's horns, and blurted out, "What exactly do I mean to you? We uh…could have…you know… So, am I just one of your fun adventures, just a glorified plaything?"

I held my breath for her answer, while we lifted the kayak and placed it on the ground. I couldn't meet her eyes. I'd just had an epiphany. I did not want to be simply a roll in the hay. I wanted something more, something I probably didn't think was possible, but I wanted it anyway. It was too bad that my talents as a Dream Weaver did not extend to making a life with Maya more than a fantasy—a living, breathing, dream.

Her finger tipped my chin, as she forced me to look at her. "You could never be a plaything, Heaven. I thought you understood that. Now, of course, it wouldn't be prudent to let Leah in on our little secret. She knows I care for you. I wasn't able to mask that completely, but she has no idea of the depth. We may be living on borrowed time, and I'm done playing the dutiful sister. From now on, I've decided it's time to start making our own plans for the future. If Leah's ideas fit, so be it. If not, we'll design our own, and I'll take Darla up on her generous offer of assistance."

For the third time, I ignored the offhand comment about Darla, because I liked the sound of the first part of what she'd said. I pulled her in my arms and gave her the most searing kiss I could. I think it was pretty spectacular for both of us, because when we broke apart, we were both panting. "Just don't tip me over, that would not be in my plans for the future."

Maya grinned at me, then reached into the car to remove the life vests. She tossed the bulky yellow jacket that had me thinking of SpongeBob SquarePants and motioned for me to put it on. "Can you grab the paddles from the back seat, please?"

"Sure." I was feeling so good that I wasn't nervous about kayaking for the first time anymore. Suddenly, I wanted to try a whole lot of new things. As long as Maya was with me, I'd do just about anything shy of jumping out of an airplane.

"We can do that next week if you want." Maya smirked.

"Stop reading my damn mind, or teach me how to read yours, so that I know when you're teasing. You have a decidedly big advantage over me. You seem to always catch me in weak moments when I am putty in your hands. I don't even try to keep your probing out like I do with Leah."

"I know." She chuckled.

"Oh, and for the record, I will never jump from a plane, not even for you."

"We'll see. It's on my bucket list."

†

We were cruising along in the water, and I was proud of myself, because I was starting to get the hang of things. My paddle slid through the water with ease, and we were making

157

progress toward Baby Island. Maya had packed a nice picnic lunch and told me that often the seals would hang out on the small beach.

They were my undoing, the baby seals. They were so darned cute when they stuck their little noses up out of the water. Bald, little puppy dogs is what they looked like to me. I was so excited when I saw them start to play with one another that I guess I leaned too far in one direction.

"Arghhhhh," I screamed, as I felt the ice-cold water of the sound. It didn't matter that Maya performed a perfect roll and we were upright within seconds. I couldn't breathe. The stunning chill knocked the air out of my lungs. I sputtered and my teeth began chattering. We were so close to Baby Island. Maya made a beeline for the beach, while I expressed my displeasure for having experienced, firsthand, the frigid water temperature.

"We need to get to the beach and change into some dry clothes before you catch your death of cold."

"You th…think?" I managed through my chattering teeth.

Maya started chuckling, while I glared at her. After learning about the yellow and red and white floats marking the various locations where a pot was waiting for unsuspecting Dungeness crabs, there was no way I was sticking my feet into the shallow waters on the shoreline of our lunch destination.

She gracefully oozed her body out of the kayak, barely rocking it, and pulled the boat onto the beach.

"Come on out, you're safe now. They don't crawl up on the beach to nibble your toes. Besides, I think they prefer turkey legs."

I shimmied out and knew that if I had exited the kayak while it was still in the water, I would have taken another involuntary swim in the sound. It wasn't my fault, kayaks are especially wobbly in the water. I didn't know how Maya could do it and barely cause a ripple.

While I was struggling to free myself from the fiberglass coffin, Maya had already popped open one of the watertight storage areas and hauled the dry bag onto the rocky beach.

"Do you mind getting us some dry clothes?" She pointed to the thick plastic bag, then began to pull out our lunch, which I sincerely hoped had not been waterlogged.

I staggered over and pushed the clip to begin unrolling the top of the bag where the design created an airtight seal. I fumbled with the damn thing, but managed to remove the extra set of clothes Maya had packed. Had she known we would go overboard?

"D…did y…you know w…we were g…going t…to t…tip?" My hands were shaking uncontrollably, as I tried to unbutton my jeans. The wet denim made it particularly difficult.

Maya ignored my question, as she dumped the last of the packed gear on the ground and pushed my hand aside. She made quick work of undoing my pants. It was then that I realized we were not the only people relaxing on Baby Island, and clearly, I was hesitant to shed my clothes and show off my bare ass to a bunch of strangers.

Maya pre-empted my protests with an order to strip. "Modesty has no place in the scheme of things when you're on the verge of hypothermia. Strip right now and get those warm clothes on your body, pronto."

As if she needed to demonstrate what I should to do, she pulled off her own wet clothes in record time and had donned the dry set so quickly, I barely saw her creamy breasts.

I shrugged. My self-consciousness wasn't all that important if it meant I would remain chilled to the bone in my sopping wet clothes.

She grabbed my hand and led me over to a log. She helped me sit with my back against the smooth driftwood, while she wrapped a blanket around me that she had retrieved from another bag. Eventually my teeth stopped chattering, and I could feel my limbs again. "How come the water didn't send you into a tailspin?"

"I belong to the Polar Bear club. In the middle of the winter, we take a plunge in the sound for kicks."

"Do you have some kind of death wish?"

"Nope, I have a life wish. Every day is a gift, Heaven. Every day you are vertical, you need to be thankful that you get to be on this planet and experience the wonders all around us."

"You are a wonder."

Her face lit up and she smiled at me. "So are you, Heaven, so much more than you give yourself credit for." She jumped up and grabbed the small cooler. "Time to eat, I'm starved. Let's see what Hana packed for us."

I was eager to see for myself. I'd never had a Japanese picnic lunch and wondered if sushi traveled well in a cooler, stuffed in a kayak, bouncing around like those ping pong balls at the church bingo halls.

I was disappointed that what was carefully laid out in the cooler was something that looked like a bento box with teriyaki chicken, rice, salmon, and tempura shrimp. I could eat sushi every single day.

Maya began to laugh. "Stop pouting. I take it this is not exactly the lunch you were hoping for."

"Wasn't there any sushi left?" I asked hopefully.

"I seem to recall the vast amounts you ate last night. Impressive. I don't think Hana was prepared for that level of enthusiasm for her delicacies. I think she believed that someone had starved you. While this isn't sushi, I guarantee you will like it."

I flipped open the lid to the condiment nestled next to the tempura and grabbed a piece of shrimp, dipping it into the brown sauce. After taking a bite and letting the flavors burst in my mouth, I moaned in pleasure. "Oh my God, that is so good."

Maya followed my lead and took her own bite. "Oh yes, it is. I don't know how she makes the tempura batter, but it is so light. The best I've ever had. At least my sister knows how to hire great chefs."

"You and your sister seem to knock heads a lot. Why?"

Maya sighed. "Ultimately, we are both aligned on the end goal, we just have different perspectives on how to get there. Before we decided to bring you into the fold, I followed along blindly, not knowing the extent of her plans. She metes out little bits of information, without giving anyone the full picture. I wish I could penetrate her blocks as easily as yours."

"Hey now. I wish I could enter your space just a tad, then I could understand why you feel you need to lie to me."

She seemed shocked by my declaration. "I haven't lied to you, Heaven. Well, not exactly."

"Haven't you ever heard of lies of omission? Failing to share small idiosyncrasies is one thing, keeping me from the big things is another." I stabbed a piece of teriyaki chicken and shoved it in my mouth.

"Define big things."

While I was chewing my food, a notion popped into my head, and I blurted it out, "You're more powerful than Leah, and somehow, you've been able to hide that from both your father and your sister."

Maya's eyes went wide. "How…how did you know that?"

I shrugged. "I don't know. I guess you must have telegraphed it. You don't like it, do you? That's why you don't want anyone to know. You think it's too easy to abuse the power, because Leah does it all the time, right?"

"Oh Heaven, I do it all the time. I abuse my power without even thinking, like when I know what you're thinking. I shouldn't be there—thoughts are private. Yet I slip in without even realizing it sometimes. I have a whole lot better control with everyone else, but somehow, I can't help myself with you. I have to use all my powers of concentration not to inadvertently enter inside your head."

"I know. At least you respected my memories of Rosie," I whispered.

"I had to work very hard against my curiousness about her. She was someone important to you."

I nodded. "She was, and I do appreciate how you let me tell you about her in my own way, in my own time."

"It was almost impossible to control myself."

"Why?"

Maya shrugged. "She's the competition."

"She's dead. She died a long time ago."

"Not in your heart. She'll never die there. That's the real reason you conjure up those ridiculous strippers and pole dancers. They'd never be able to take Rosie's place. I couldn't bear being in the same category as one of them."

"Don't worry, you'd never be in that category. Your clothes aren't revealing enough, and no offense, but you're not a double D," I teased.

"You wanted honesty. If you can't stand the heat, don't build the fire."

"Fair enough. How about we finish eating this wonderful food, pack up, and brave the waves of death. I'm a bit of a processor, and I need a little time to readjust my thinking. I've sort of convinced myself that entering into any kind of relationship with a freak like me would be the very definition of a disaster. But seeing as how you're kinda in my same freakish league, who knows, things might be worth taking a serious second peek at the options. Of course, that probably won't happen until we resolve your daddy issues."

Maya laughed. "Now you sound like my shrink."

"You have a shrink?"

"Well, no, but if I did have one, I'm sure they would use the very same vernacular—daddy issues."

"Right you are. I don't think that Baby Island is the place to enter into a deep discussion about anything, but I do expect to learn a little more about you and your life experiences, considering I've given you a considerable glimpse into how I evolved to the person I am today."

"I will, I promise. Timing is everything," she murmured.

I was thankful our conversation remained light, as we finished our lunch. I had a lot to think about, but for the rest of the afternoon, we stuck to our agreement to keep things fluffy.

On our return journey, Maya reminded me that if I wanted to stay dry, I needed to refrain from becoming too enamored with the seals or the orcas, should one choose to bless us with its presence. I sputtered when she mentioned the large mammal might do a swim by and nearly tipped us over again, but Maya managed to keep us upright.

†

At the same time that I felt a jolt of fear, Maya glanced at me as we came within a mile of Leah's house. Something was clearly wrong. A barrage of frantic thoughts with a healthy dose of terror nearly stifled my ability to breathe.

"What the hell is happening to me?"

Maya brought the SUV to a screeching halt about a half mile away from her sister's sanctuary. Her puzzled look did not settle my rising panic. "What exactly are you feeling? Are you hearing anyone's thoughts?"

I grabbed my head hoping to make it stop. *Help, help. I'll teach that bitch. Don't let her get in your head. Where are Heaven and Maya? Please stop, please stop, I'll tell you anything you want to know...* I rattled off the running commentary in my head, until it became too jumbled to separate the individual orders and pleas that I knew were coming from more than one person.

"Breathe, Heaven, and concentrate on just one voice. Can you pick out just one? Together, we can search for Leah. Open your mind to her thoughts and block out the others. She can project more easily to us without overwhelming your senses."

I imagined separating several strings of Christmas lights, until I held one in my hand. *Turn around, Syl...* Pain, incredible pain flooded my body, then nothing. An eerie blankness.

"It's okay, Heaven. They've neutralized her. The new drugs are very hard to defend against."

The next thought sent a shiver through my body, *Reprogram those four and use the new drugs on Leah. I'm done playing games. When you find Maya and Heaven, if you can't turn them, put them in the Dream Pod. No excuses. I don't give a fuck about the instability. If it fries their brains, so be it.*

"Shit," Maya mumbled.

"What is the Dream Pod?"

"Something neither one of us want to get up close and personal with. Not one single Weaver or Catcher has come away unharmed. The most common reaction is a complete brain wipe. We'd be nothing more than a human vegetable, but even that outcome is preferred over the alternative."

"The alternative?"

"A perpetual loop of your worst nightmare. Whatever monster you conjure up ends up chasing you in your dream for the rest of your life, until your heart finally gives out."

"Do you think Syl turned on us?"

"No, I don't. I know it might sound like Leah was warning us about Syl. I can't explain how I know Syl is on our side, but I do. I think it's a safe bet that they've taken everyone captive. This time, they'll not make the same errors in judgment they did when Leah launched her plan. They do have some inside help. I'm sure of it, but I don't believe it's Syl. I also don't believe the help was voluntarily offered. The more likely candidates are Brenda and Star. They wouldn't have suspected we would venture out today. I think they believed you and I were more damaged than we were."

"So, what do we do now?"

"See if Syl and Darla got away and pulled together reinforcements, then we attack. My father has no idea about the army Darla and I trained while Leah and the rest were working with my father's recruits. See, Leah is a snob who never bothered much with low-level Catchers and Weavers. She thought they weren't worth the effort. My father's rejects."

"They're all like you, aren't they? Darla has an army?" The little hints about Darla were starting to make sense now.

Maya smiled. "Deception and subterfuge aren't always negative traits. Add a little love and respect, and the paired teams will be unstoppable."

"How come you never tried to shut down your father before now?"

"I hadn't met the yin to my yang." She reached over and stroked my face. "I wish we had more time to find our synergy, but I'm afraid our timeline has shortened."

The enormity of what we were about to embark upon created a huge pit in my stomach. I didn't think I had the strength or requisite talent to win this war. It was a battle I didn't start and wanted no part in, but Maya seemed to have faith in me, and I didn't want to let her down.

"You could never let me down, Heaven. You are my yin. I knew it the moment I laid eyes on you and felt your energy."

"How come you didn't say anything before?"

"You weren't ready to hear that, and I couldn't take the chance you would turn away from me. So, I had to temper my emotions. It was the hardest thing I've ever had to do."

"The monsters that originate out of my mind are truly horrendous sometimes. I don't want to live the rest of my life in a never-ending nightmare. Is it okay to be scared?"

"Yes, it is. Remember when I said you had a hole in your knowledge base?"

I nodded.

"When a Weaver connects with a Catcher who is their yin or yang, the control of the apparitions that the Weaver conjures is amplified to such a great degree, the pair can almost operate as one. You know how your emotions affect the strength of your dreams and that in turn causes whatever you create to come to life and stay in the here and now for a short period. That period of time increases as the level of your emotion increases. Catchers were created to control those emotions and subsequently, the dream apparitions."

"I don't quite understand how it works. I know the drugs amplified my dreams and helped to bring them to life, but I don't understand how Catchers are able to control my creations."

"Leah has tried to enter your head on numerous occasions. You've felt the tickle and you block it. You haven't blocked me, even though I have tried very hard not to be invasive when I've penetrated your mind. Catchers get inside a Weaver's head, and that's how they are able to help control the apparitions," Maya patiently explained.

"You absorb my thoughts and feelings?"

Maya nodded. "Sort of. It's more like I link with you."

"Then you feel my fear? I don't want you to absorb that fear."

Maya shook her head and touched my cheek. "Oh, my beautiful Heaven, it's okay. Believe it or not, sometimes fear helps us sharpen our edge. The trick is not to let fear overwhelm you and cause inertia."

"You're always going to be there to push me to the edge, aren't you?"

"Yes, always."

Maya turned her face forward, put the car in gear, and made a quick U-turn. We screeched in the opposite direction of my temporary safe haven. I worried about the group of women I had barely started to bond with. I hadn't spent enough time to truly feel a part of the team, but that didn't mean I wanted to let them rot in Dr. Spartan's lab of terrors, controlled by Maya's father. I couldn't understand how someone so good like Maya shared the same genes as someone so evil.

Would I ever have roots? Would I ever feel safe and settled?

CHAPTER NINETEEN

As we drove along, the landscape transformed into something wilder and much less populated. The trees definitely outnumbered the houses. Maya turned onto a gravel road that seemed to go on forever. The silence in the car amplified the crunching sound that the tires made, as we traveled slowly up the long, winding road.

Maya had been contemplative the whole way over, and I'd decided to leave her to her thoughts. I could ask more questions later. I remained in the passenger seat, quiet and subdued, but not depressed. That was an anomaly. Usually when I was afraid, I went into a dark place. I didn't have gray in my wheelhouse, only black and white. Either I was bouncing off the walls with excitement and white light shooting from my pores, or I was locked inside a dark, black dungeon, oozing tar from every orifice in my body. I didn't have time to consider this new development, as we approached our destination.

Around the last bend, I got my first glimpse of the educational campus that I would later name, Dream Seekers' Commune. My perspective would never be the same after spending time in this magical place. Everything changed for me there.

The most astonishing thing was the neat rows of dwellings that looked like tiny houses. I'd read about tiny houses, and I wanted to take a tour. The story had fascinated me, because I thought I'd be particularly suited to something like that. I'd never needed a lot of room. A bed, a microwave, and a place to sit and read while drinking coffee in the morning were all I ever required.

"Are those tiny houses?" I couldn't contain my excitement.

A slow grin formed on Maya's face. "They are."

"Can we take a tour? I've heard about them, and I always wanted to take a peek inside one. I think they are the coolest things."

"Maybe later." She came to a complete stop in front of a large, wooden structure. I wasn't sure if it was a house or some kind of recreation center. It looked almost as massive as Leah's place. "Come on, let's see if Syl made it here and if they are already starting to pull everyone together.

I followed her lead and undid my seatbelt, scrambling out of the car and hurrying to follow her sure, confident, footsteps to the massive front door. The swirling pattern in the grain seemed to stand out, and I wondered how the builder accomplished that. Had they used a natural stain like linseed oil, or was it something special? I was following the designs, tracing them to their origins, when Maya grabbed my hand and pulled open the door.

"I've never seen a door so beautiful," I said.

She chuckled. "Every single thing about Darla's refuge was planned to the tiniest detail. She wanted us to surround ourselves with everything that elicits tranquility and confidence."

The cavernous space inside the large structure created a warm, comfortable feeling. There was a large fireplace off to the side. I imagined each stone that surrounded the opening was lovingly placed by the mason who'd crafted it. When I looked up, there were massive wood beams with the same beautiful grain patterns that I'd seen in the front door.

I'm not sure where Darla and Syl came from, but they suddenly appeared in front of us and their smiles were genuine. Darla reached for Maya first and hugged her, then placed a kiss on her cheek, while Syl grabbed me and offered a desperate hug. I knew I shouldn't let the dark emotion sneak in, but a twinge of jealousy caused me to narrow my eyes, as Darla finally released Maya. When Maya stroked my arm, those feelings dissipated immediately.

"I knew you would escape," Darla said.

"It was just dumb luck, really. Maya took me kayaking. When we were headed back and got close to the house, I felt something."

"Nothing that happens in the universe is dumb luck, Heaven. Something told Maya to remove you from danger." Darla pointed to the comfortable sofa and chairs surrounding the fireplace. "Come, sit down, and we can fill in the gaps before bringing the troops together."

I knew that Darla was Syl's girlfriend, but I hadn't spent a lot of time around the two of them. Since Syl had taken me in, I tried to make myself scarce whenever Darla came over, because they appeared to never have enough time together. Besides she'd acted so pissed about the pole dancer, but maybe it was just that, all an act.

I scrutinized Syl, as we made our way to the fire. She looked different. She was almost glowing and seemed far less like herself. Sometimes, Syl tried to carry the weight of the world on her shoulders and wore a pained expression more often than one of joy. She'd make the perfect mother, always looking like she was concerned about her children.

I sat on one of the love seats and Maya joined me. When I turned my attention to Darla, I blurted out my sudden realization that this group of women were masters of deception. "You weren't upset at all when I dreamed up that pole dancer and she shimmied up to Syl. Wow, you acted all mad for a full two weeks. Gotta give you props for those acting skills. You must have all studied under the same theatre instructor." I was surprised I noted this without a hint of bitterness. It was merely an observation.

Darla leaned forward. "I take full responsibility, Heaven. Maya went along with my assessment. I felt you needed a bit more time before we revealed everything to you. So yes, it was all a ruse to appear as though Leah wanted to connect you to Maya. Even Syl hadn't been completely briefed until today. It caused a bit of a rift in our relationship, however we are a strong couple who love each other. Love will always prevail. But, never question that we all care about you and the other innocent women who've suffered under Dr. Spartan's program."

"Syl, did you rescue me from the lab, just so I could join the cause?" I asked.

Syl looked away. "I met Leah several years ago. She has incredible persuasive powers. At the time, I was a promising scientist in the study of sleep disorders. She convinced me to join Spartan's team and become her inside person."

She turned her gaze back to me and met my eyes. "There was subterfuge involved. I'm sorry. When I joined Spartan's team, I had to suffer through the abuse I witnessed every single day. Even if Leah had not told me about you, I would have recognized how special you are. The deception does not mean I didn't ultimately have your best interests in mind. After I met Darla, I decided to speed up Leah's timeline. I didn't realize how much Darla helped me break my connection to Leah, nor did I know the full extent of the plan." Syl's eyes shifted to Darla's, and I got the sense that there was still a bit of tenderness around that lie of omission.

"I'm sorry, my love. That will remain the biggest regret of my life." Darla looked away.

Syl turned her head back and captured her eyes. The love was so evident on Syl's face. "You're forgiven, so it's time to forgive yourself. We need your strength. I suppose I should thank Leah for introducing me to Darla. Even though Leah never thought much of Darla's skills, I knew she was extraordinary the moment I met her. As remarkable as you are, Heaven, but in a much different way."

Maya took my hand. "I should have come clean that very first day you came to my house. I'm sorry. I knew the instant I met you, we would be a formidable pair, but you were still working on ridding your body of the drugs and figuring out the limits of your gift. I knew it wasn't the right time."

I contemplated how much my moods had leveled out, without drugs, since meeting Maya, and I wanted to know why. It wasn't like I missed the highs and lows, because I hadn't experienced the flat affect the drugs caused. It was merely a curiosity. "How come I don't need the meds to level me out anymore?"

"Maya is your matched half. She fits like Rosie. In some ways, the fit is tighter than with Rosie, because you were so young before and still needed to grow," Darla began.

At the mention of Rosie, I stiffened, and Maya squeezed my hand for reassurance.

"Think of how a person changes and grows through childhood and puberty. Sometimes people are lucky to find that right person in adolescence and they come together nicely, others seem to reject the partners of their youth, because the seams no longer match up. After a person develops fully, the connection with their matched pair is tight. Of course, this is not always the case. There are those rare circumstances when a person is a very late bloomer and dramatic change still occurs midlife," Darla patiently explained.

A burst of hope flooded my body. I realized that I did not have to navigate my way through the world alone anymore. "So, are you saying that as long as I stay connected to Maya, I won't need medication?"

A trio of smiles lit up the room, as Syl nodded and Darla affirmed my supposition.

"Yes, that is exactly what I am saying," Darla confirmed.

"And Maya, you'll stick with me?" I tentatively asked.

"Of course. A person never passes up the gift of finding their matched pair," Maya answered.

I wasn't sure how to ask the next question, especially in front of Syl and Darla. "Um, so do matched pairs always, uh…you know…"

"Yes, almost always. There are rare occasions when physical intimacy is not a part of the pairing, but unless you would prefer otherwise, that would not be the case for us." Maya turned her face to mine and the smoldering look she gave me was enough to make me want to drag her to the nearest bedroom. Maybe we could find an empty bed in one of those tiny houses. That would be a nice fantasy come true.

"Have we answered your burning questions?" Darla asked.

I nodded. "For now, yeah. I have more, but I can ask later." I wanted to learn more about how Darla hooked up with Syl and the specific plans they'd cooked up, but I didn't have a burning desire to know the answers at that moment. I'd never pegged Darla for a Catcher or a Weaver, but she was definitely a leader. She had a quiet, commanding style that made everyone listen, even when she whispered her commands.

"Good. I prefer the just-in-time approach to the fire hose."

I scrunched up my face to Darla's response.

"Provide you with only the information you need at this particular time, a dribble of water to quench your thirst, versus blasting you with too much information that will only overwhelm you like water from a fire hose."

That made sense to me, and I felt myself relax and sit back in the love seat. "So, when do I get to meet the rest of the raggedy bunch of Weavers and Catchers? Can I take a tour of one of those tiny houses? Do I get assigned one of my own?" I asked excitedly.

"You'd rather stay in one of those dwellings instead of here at the main complex?" Syl asked.

"Well, yeah. I'd rather not hear you and Darla in the throes of passion every single night," I quipped.

"I'll move my stuff into Number 15. That's empty, right?" Maya asked.

Darla waved her hand in the air. "Whatever is most comfortable for you is fine by me. Syl, do you want to gather the troops for introductions?"

†

Syl left to collect our mini-army while Darla led us to a large space that looked vaguely like a conference room but was less institutional than the kind of business facility that had long tables with a projector hanging from the ceiling that a person could connect a laptop to. The tables were finely grained wood, and an eclectic collection of artwork hung on the walls. The stark contrast of the technology showcased on one wall with the almost homey atmosphere of the room, was fascinating to me. I suppose some people might think the room had too many dissimilarities to succeed, but I thought it worked just fine.

Twenty women shuffled into the room and took seats at the various tables. I was amazed at the variety. Not only did their body types run the gamut, but there were all ages and many different races. Their one similarity struck me; I'd seen the same trait in Syl, Maya, and Darla. All of the women held this air of serenity and confidence. I wanted to emulate that.

"You do," Maya whispered in my ear.

I wasn't really serious when I leaned over and responded, "Stop burrowing in my head." She chuckled. Somehow, she

176

managed to only capture my thoughts when they weren't so private that I felt violated.

A woman of generous proportions strolled over and sat on the other side of me. Next to her sat a tall, thin bean pole. I could tell they were a matched pair and thought they looked a bit like the female version of Laurel and Hardy—but friendlier than the pompous Hardy.

The ample-breasted woman leaned close to me and whispered, "Hello, you must be Heaven. We are so excited to meet you. I'm Gretchen, and this is Beanie. That's her nickname. She doesn't mind people calling her that; she barely even remembers her Christian name." Gretchen's deep dimples made an appearance on her full face.

I chuckled to myself after hearing her nickname and was sure I knew the reason people called her that. I grinned at her. "Hi, glad to meet you." Beanie waved at me. I liked them right off. In less than ten seconds, I'd developed more of a bond with Gretchen and Beanie than I had with Leah's group.

"You look so good together. We are so happy that Maya found her match. She's been so lost lately. We could tell right away after she met you," Beanie remarked.

I wondered when Maya had slipped away since we met. I could only think of the first night, when she went home and arranged for me to come to her place the next day. Had she known then?

Darla stood up and cleared her throat. She had a commanding presence, yet subtle compared to Leah. I got the sense that although Darla was certainly a leader and maybe even the guru to this group of women, Maya's talents and mentorship probably surpassed Darla's.

"I'd like you all to introduce yourselves. Just give the basics, your name, your primary skill, in other words whether you are a Weaver or Catcher, and how long you've lived here."

I wasn't even going to try to remember everyone's name. I almost suggested we plaster those little, paper name tags on our chests, but that seemed like new-employee orientation, and what we were about to embark on was considerably more serious than starting a new job.

I sat there quietly, soaking in the positive energy, while everyone introduced themselves. Then it came to my turn. "Hi everyone, I'm Heavenlaya, but everyone calls me Heaven. Um…I guess I'm more of a Weaver, at least that's what I've always assumed, until I learned I could tap into my inner Catcher with Maya's assistance. I've lived here for thirty minutes."

That generated a chuckle from everyone.

"I think everyone knows me already." Maya turned her face toward me. "It's not a stupid idea, Heaven."

"Huh?" I responded.

Maya returned her attention to Darla. "Twenty names are a lot to remember. Could we bring out the name tags?"

Beanie clapped her hands. "Oh, yes, I don't mind wearing them, even if it's only for Heaven's benefit. We need to do everything we can to make her feel comfortable. Don't you agree, Darla?"

Darla's trademark slow smile appeared. "I do. Syl can you grab the name tags I had made for today?"

Syl laughed. "Figures. You probably had them specially made. Are they in one of the cabinets?"

Darla nodded. "Don't you think these amazing women deserve individualized name badges?"

Syl opened the rich, wood cabinet and started to pull out boxes. She peeked inside two, before pulling out a small box. She walked to the tables and began handing out the engraved tags. When she placed mine in front of me, I was surprised. Was Darla a seer who knew this day would come and I would join this group of unlikely saviors? I looked at my tag and saw a rainbow attached to a cloud next to the words, *Dream Warriors*. Was I really a warrior? On the second line was my name—just my first name, *Heaven*. I suppose when facing danger, it doesn't really matter if you know the last names of your comrades.

When I put on the name tag, I felt pride. I was a part of something larger than myself.

Gretchen brushed her fingers across her own tag. "These are nice. How come we never had these before?" she said without a hint of animosity. I sensed that she was genuinely curious, not jealous or upset.

"We've already eased into comfortable working relationships with one another. I thought this might help Heaven feel a part of the team as its newest member," Darla answered.

I could see many of the women nod their heads, and others blurted out various affirmations like, "oh yes," and "good idea."

Gretchen and Beanie both whispered in unison, "We're so glad you're here."

Syl walked over to Darla and kissed her on the cheek, "That's why I love you so much. You are always thinking of other people and their feelings. I really do forgive you, my love."

I could see Darla relax even more, almost like a large boulder had fallen off her shoulder. I don't think there was ever a time in my life when I'd felt so good about myself. This was a loving family. They could depend on me, and I could count on them.

"When can we rescue Leah and the rest of our team?" I asked. I was anxious to get the show on the road. I was ready for action.

Darla and Syl exchanged a strange look, and I sensed their unease. All the other women looked down.

"May I?" Maya interjected. "We will be taking action, but Leah and her group… Well, they are not exactly part of our team."

A muscular woman with a tattoo sleeve blurted out, "Leah calls us rejects."

I squinted my eyes, so I could cheat and read her name. I didn't think Catrina fit her, but then I didn't think Heaven fit me either.

"Leah's a bitch," Beanie whispered.

It was the first negative thing she'd said since I'd met her.

"It doesn't matter what Leah thinks of us. Ultimately, we have the same goal, and they're in trouble." Darla shifted uncomfortably.

"I wasn't suggesting that we shouldn't save their asses, just filling in the blanks for Heaven," Catrina said.

"Yeah, me too. Just stating a fact, sorry Maya," Beanie agreed.

I turned to Maya. "How come you took me to Leah's place instead of here? I like it better here. It fits."

A vehement round of affirmations resonated in the air. "Damn straight," and "Fuck yes."

"You were on Leah's radar, and she would have made Darla and Syl's lives miserable if I didn't deposit you on her doorstep. I knew it was inevitable that we would need to work together, so I was biding my time until everything aligned. I let her believe what she wanted. Unfortunately, we've had some developments that neither group anticipated." Maya looked at me apologetically.

"Her fault with her half-baked plan," I grumbled.

"On the bright side, her plan has quickened the original timeline. I had intended to bring you here after your initial training with Leah. I knew she would immediately recognize that we were a match but would still insist you stay at her compound to receive what she believes is superior training. I think it was a blow to her ego that you and she were not a match. It was always in the cards for us to end up here."

"That ought to wipe that haughty smirk off Leah's face, the rejects and Heaven saving their sorry asses," Catrina added.

Darla glanced over at Catrina. "Be careful not to take a page in Leah's book," she gently chastised. "We won't be able to act until Syl has the formula to counteract their latest drug. How long will you need?"

"Maybe two more days," Syl answered.

Maya frowned. "I'm not sure some of them have that long. Leah maybe, but she, like the rest, is completely expendable. He was willing and ready to let us both die."

"We're dead in the water, unless we can counteract the serum that blunts our skills. Any chance you can speed up the process, hon?" Darla asked.

"I'll do the best I can."

"The rest of us need to continue our exercises, rest, and be ready on a moment's notice. I want everyone to pair up and hone your skills. Don't practice to the point of exhaustion, because we need everyone fresh and ready for battle. At least all of you are familiar with the Dream Center. I'd like to work with a small group who believes they know the layout better than the rest of you. I would imagine that he let some of you roam freer than others, because he'd determined you were not a threat. Those of you who snuck around unnoticed and managed to create a blueprint in your brain are the ones I need to work with on our entry plan." Darla shifted her eyes around the room.

I shook my head. "Don't look at me. They barely let me out of confinement."

Maya stood, then gently took my arm and lifted me up. "What do you say to a tour of the tiny house and a few exercises to hone your skills?" She punctuated her suggestion with a smile.

I was excited to see one of the cottages. If I'd heard correctly, Maya and I were assigned to Number 15. She slung her arm around my shoulder, and we left the large conference room in search of our temporary residence.

I was getting used to being a nomad. Other than the short detour back to Spartan's lair, the places I'd been staying over the last few weeks were relatively luxurious.

"Does it have a tiny shower?" I asked with enthusiasm.

Maya chuckled, as she led me outside into the warmth of the sunshine. "As a matter of fact, I do believe it does."

"Brilliant."

CHAPTER TWENTY

The tiny house was made of cedar, and it smelled so nice. I vaguely remembered my grandmother's cedar chest. I used to lift the lid where she kept all the linens, because I liked to smell the cedar. It never seemed to lose that clean, fresh scent that filled the room and reminded me of her love.

I wondered if the death of my grandparents was what triggered the first depressive episode. I think I'd read somewhere that traumatic events could cause the first onset. I was sure that was what had happened; I'd experienced symptoms several years before adolescent-onset bipolar disorder normally appeared.

Maya opened the door to a cozy room, with a soft, cinnamon-colored sofa accented with earth-toned pillows. The residence wasn't very wide, and I could see all the way to the queen size bed at the other end of the house. I guessed that it was no more than 300 square feet. The compact kitchen was right there in the main living area, and I suspected the tiny shower was probably a few feet away next to the bedroom. There was a door that separated the kitchen/living room from the bedroom, which basically had the bed and built in closet, with dressers on both sides.

I headed for the bedroom and saw the shower to the left. The small bathroom on the right was complete with a toilet and vanity. Bouncing on the bed, I checked out the mattress and was surprised by the quality. This was going to be a very comfortable place to sleep, or enjoy other recreational activities. I could feel my face flush, as I thought about Maya and me sharing this space.

Maya's hearty laugh broke my lascivious thoughts, "Well, what do you think?"

"I love it. I could totally see myself living here." I turned my face to look at her. "Do you think that is at all possible…you know…after we uh take care of…"

"You want to live with a bunch of other women, here?"

"You think it's a stupid idea." My head dropped.

Maya sat next to me on the bed. "No, not at all. I feel more comfortable here among the positive energy of the other Weavers and Catchers than at Leah's large estate, or even my humble home. Darla has created a perfect space. I just didn't think anyone else would share my vision of family."

"It's been forever since I felt like I was part of any family. Syl's been the closest thing lately, but I could tell something was amiss. She seems way more comfortable here with Darla than I ever noticed when we lived together."

"Darla has a way of creating a nice safe space and bringing to the surface everyone's natural goodness."

"Darla's not a Catcher or a Weaver, right?"

"No, she has other special gifts, just like Syl."

"You mean like her ability to lead a ragtag team of Weavers and Catchers?"

"Yes. Every one of the Dream Warriors would follow her into the depths of hell if she asked. Myself included."

"I've been there and back. On multiple occasions. Every time I sink into a depression, I bring back the monsters from hell."

"It won't always be like that for you."

I hopped up off the bed. "We should probably do our exercises, or whatever we're supposed to be doing now, to get ready for the big confrontation."

"Confrontation. I like that better than war. Okay. Let's head out to the living room."

The house might have been compact, but the couch was top of the line and extremely comfortable. I eased my way to the couch first. Maya sat next to me, but turned her body so that we could almost touch foreheads without being awkward.

"You're not going to make me dream up a flame again, are you?"

"No, we need to start working together to create something powerful enough to use against my father and his vast security personnel, without harming the innocent residents of the center."

"How do we do that? You know my biggest, baddest monsters are very indiscriminate about who they go after."

"That's why we are more powerful together. Your strength is your creativity and mine is control and focus."

Maya jumped up and ran out of the house. I was so confused. *What did I do wrong, already? Am I supposed to follow her?* She hadn't said a word, so I just sat there, dumbfounded.

†

A few minutes passed in silence, as I continued to sit in the tiny house on the comfortable sofa. I decided to poke around a bit and see what was hiding in the cabinets. I was especially curious about the drawers on each side of the bed. When I pulled open one of the compartments on the right, I found it stuffed full of thongs. Interesting.

I pulled open the solid wood doors on the left side of the nearly full-sized refrigerator. I found a small pantry loaded with cans and boxes. Just as I was about to snack on some granola mix, Maya burst through the door carrying a large, fluffy, gray cat with an adorable white muzzle.

I didn't know why she'd left to gather this cat, but I didn't care. I love cats so, I reached out to pet his head. I assumed it was male, because he was huge. His purr was so loud, I could almost feel it reverberate up my arm.

"Oh, aren't you a handsome fellow," I crooned.

Maya laughed. "Well I suppose Cleopatra is a bit butch, but she's all female."

"She's the biggest cat I've ever seen." Seeing Cleopatra made me miss my buddy, Satan. I wondered if Syl had brought him to the compound and if he was friends with Cleopatra.

Maya scratched her chin. "Don't listen to her Cleo. You're not fat. You're fluffy."

I continued to pet Cleo. "I did not say you were fat. There is a big difference between big and overweight." I looked up at Maya. "Not that I mind you bringing a cat to me, but why is she here?"

"The exercise we are going to do doesn't necessarily require Cleo's expertise, but she will definitely help us refine our skill."

"Do you know if Syl brought Satan here? He can be ornery, but he's a good boy. I think he would get along with Cleo."

"Satan was out back stalking a mouse. He definitely wasn't interested in being picked up."

"Too bad. I miss the little bugger."

"Hmmm, maybe next time, he can participate. Two might be better than one."

I was intrigued. What was Maya up to? I liked her spontaneity; most of her activities were fun. Although I can't say I liked the candle thing.

"You've definitely piqued my curiosity."

"Cleo loves to chase a laser pointer. She'll do that for hours, if I keep it up. Creating a small beam of light and moving it with precision to keep a cat entertained is more difficult than you'd think. We'll start with one point of light that we generate together. After we are proficient enough to entertain Cleo, we'll drive her crazy with two lights that will eventually combine to one." Maya set Cleo down on the floor, and the cat began to weave in and out of Maya's legs until she sat down.

I sat next to Maya, and Cleo jumped up and settled into her lap.

"So how exactly do we do this?"

"Imagining is really the very same process every time." Maya grabbed my hand. "Together, we need to concentrate on creating a small dot that resembles a laser beam. The hard part will be making sure we both aim the dot in the same direction. Once the link is established and we are in sync, believe it or not, it is that much harder to separate our dots and then bring them back together. You ready? Imagine a small beam of light, then concentrate on what I'm thinking so we can move it together."

At first, my blue light and Maya's red light danced around the tiny house but did not seem to merge. Cleo was going crazy trying to chase both lights. I narrowed my focus and began to anticipate where she was moving the light she sent all around the small living area. Soon, our two lights came together and created a deep, purple dot. At first, the dot moved slowly as our concentration merged to create a fluid movement. We became more proficient and allowed the two lights to separate a fraction from each other and remain independent, moving gracefully together, side by side. It felt like an analogy for the perfect couple. Two independent women who move together with a common vision and goal. I wanted my life to be like that again, and it seemed like Maya might be the person to fill that void. I probably had a dopey expression on my face, as I fantasized about a possible life with Maya. My light started to grow brighter next to Maya's. Hers did as well, then they burst together in an almost neon purple light.

"That's a nice thought," Maya said.

I smiled. "Can you teach me to read your mind? I think I am at a big disadvantage here."

"It's not exactly precise. I get more pictures and feelings than words, but when those feelings are strong, the words pop in as well."

Cleo leapt up against the wall, still chasing the light, and I giggled. "Should we continue?"

Maya impulsively kissed me on the lips. "No I think that is enough of that exercise. Poor Cleo would continue to play the game until she was completely exhausted."

The purple light extinguished, and Cleo looked up at us as if we'd taken away her last friend. I leaned back against the couch with Maya, and Cleo decided we were still okay, as she jumped into my lap. I started to pet her silky fur and was more relaxed than I'd been in a very long time.

"Who does Cleo belong to?"

"Everyone, we all share in her loving attention, and she eats up all the devotion we give her. She really does match her name, because she certainly acts like an Egyptian queen."

"I'm amazed that one of my creations hasn't considered Satan a snack. I guess I never thought of the risk before, because I needed a cat to keep me company."

"I don't think you have to worry about that now. You're doing extremely well. The laser light exercise is particularly difficult, and most people can't come close to mastering it on their first try. You took to it like a duck to water."

"I did?"

"Uh huh. You should have seen me try it the first time. I couldn't create that pinpoint of light, it was more like a big spotlight that blinked on and off. It took me the longest time to make the light move in a controlled manner. I suppose it helps that we are a matched pair. I had to depend on my skill without the added energy from someone else. I've been looking for my yin for a long time."

I felt my face flush and leaned into her touch as she stroked my cheek. This kiss was more passionate, with a touch of urgency. Maya was an expert with her tongue and used it to build my arousal. Before gently sucking just a smidgeon on my bottom lip, she let her tongue caress the inside and outside of my mouth. As the heat rose, we were interrupted by a loud, "Meow."

I'd forgotten about Cleo, who had found a comfortable spot on my lap and was being crushed between us as we came together.

Maya chuckled. "Sorry my little queen. I forgot you were there. Damn, spoiled again in my attempt to seduce the lovely Heaven."

"You were trying to seduce me?"

Cleo jumped down and haughtily ran to the bed and promptly curled up next to a pillow.

"Of course. I'm not exercising any more restraint. Life's way too short." Maya shuddered. "I found that out during Leah's foolish plan. I hate that she used the affection between us even more than what I endured in that little hellhole. Letting her believe she was in control and running the show was a big misstep on my part. Darla feels responsible, but it really was my fault. It is the second biggest regret in my life."

I wanted to ask her about what happened. She'd looked like death warmed over after the rescue. I was amazed that hadn't generated one of the particularly nasty monsters that usually appeared when my emotions flared. I suppose the drugs had hampered my normal reaction. I was curious about her other big regret as well, but I didn't want to push Maya to think about painful memories.

"It's done and over with, and I don't intend on ever getting caught unawares again. Syl will perfect her serum, and that will be our defense against one of their only weapons against us," Maya answered the thoughts I'd just had about her kidnapping.

I shook my head. "I don't know, Maya, they seem to keep perfecting their own ways to control us. This last time was…"

"You're partially correct. It was an epic fail on our part, when we weren't ready. Syl was already working on the serum. I vastly underestimated my sister's lack of patience. I honestly did not believe Leah would take action as soon as she did."

"You knew she was planning to have you kidnapped?"

Maya waved her hand in the air. "Absolutely. Child's play. Leah is not as clever as she thinks she is."

"So why didn't you stop her?"

Maya frowned. "I let myself get momentarily distracted and didn't pinpoint the timeline for her plan. I'm so sorry, Heaven."

"It's okay, we got out. Your idea of fun is far more alarming to me."

Maya laughed long and hard at that.

"Oh Heaven, you are so precious. We have to work on your sense of adventure. A boring life is not a life worth living."

"Uh, I don't agree. I think I could easily live a boring life with you and be content for the rest of my life. I don't need any more excitement. I've definitely had my fair share."

"You honestly didn't have just a tiny bit of fun ziplining or kayaking?"

I paused to consider her question. *I have to admit that I did have fun, but I'm not an adrenaline junkie like Maya. I enjoyed myself, but was the elation more about the company than the activity?*

"Okay, I admit I had fun, but I draw the line at jumping out of an airplane. You're gonna have to pry my cold, dead hands from whatever I can grasp in that plane before I will ever voluntarily jump."

"We'll see."

"I'm serious, Maya. There's only so much I will agree to. Even for you. I don't understand how in the world I got paired with an adventure seeker."

"Opposites attract. That's the way of the world. It's like with magnets, the greater the opposite charge, the harder it is to break the two pieces apart."

I could feel my mouth turn upside down into a frown. "I guess you are the positive electron and I'm the negative."

Maya pulled me into a warm embrace and pecked my forehead. "No, Heaven, don't think of yourself in that manner. You are like the bright blue light you produced. Beautiful and clean, refreshing like a cool, blue lake or the sky when the sun is shining and illuminating the world in pure goodness."

She took my hand and led me to the bed. Cleo was still curled up next to the pillow, and I felt bad when Maya shooed her out but glad at the same time. This time my dream lover wasn't a figment of my overactive imagination. She was real. I was determined not to let any negative self-talk get in the way of making love with Maya.

†

The confident woman took a minivacation, as Maya looked at me almost shyly. I pushed aside any performance anxiety and mustered up a level of self-assurance I didn't know I possessed. I took the lead this time.

We both divested ourselves of our clothes, bypassing the sensual ritual of undressing the other. Honestly, untangling clothes is sometimes awkward, and I wanted skin to skin contact more quickly.

For the first time, I was truly able to connect with the emotion Maya was projecting. *Without a doubt, this is exactly what she wants, too. We are spiritually and energetically connected on a deeper level than I believed was possible. I am yin to her yang. We are that incredible, matched pair.*

Before we climbed under the covers, I asked, "Can we just pause a second? I need to look at you before I touch what is real." I'd seen her naked in the shower, but somehow, this was different. The soft light in the room created a different ambiance, and I felt a sort of reverence for the gift I was about to receive.

"I'm real, Heaven, and so is this. No more doubt. No more hesitancy."

My hand traveled from her jawline down to the curve in her waist. On the way down, I barely brushed against the sides of her breast and was rewarded with a sigh. I saw the mark again; it nearly pulsated in front of me. How could it look far angrier than it had in the shower? I traced my finger over the spot.

"When did this happen?"

She shrugged. "Compliments of my last vacation at my father's place. He wanted information, I was a bit stubborn and wouldn't tell him anything. He got angry. It's a good thing Leah and the team came to the rescue. I didn't have much time."

"How come you didn't use your skills? You're more powerful than Leah."

"Whatever new drug my father has, it is very effective at dampening my skill. Thank God Syl's serum worked on

Leah. I don't think Syl wanted everyone to be a guinea pig for the serum, so the rest of you had firsthand experience with how his methods have evolved."

"I don't understand, then how come Leah can't get away from him now?"

"I don't know." A dark look crossed Maya's face, before she seemed to shake the thought away.

I couldn't quite read the thought, but I clearly sensed disbelief. "You think she allowed herself to be taken again, don't you?"

A bitter laugh erupted from Maya. "And you think I'm the adventurous one?"

I didn't want a dark cloud to mar our first time, so I moved into a lighter path. "Does your adventurous spirit extend to the bedroom?" I asked.

Maya chuckled. "If you mean do I like to try new things? Absolutely, I'm very open to creative ways to express love, but I draw the line at physical pain. I hope that doesn't disappoint you."

I kept running my fingers lightly over her body and watched the goosebumps erupt. "Good, hard and fast isn't something I'm very fond of either. Honestly, I never could understand the notion of being fucked so hard it was uncomfortable the next day. Maybe uncomfortable because of muscles being used that haven't been exercised in a while. That will be the case with me, but sore inside…not really my cup of tea."

Maya placed her finger on my lips. "I think you might be stalling now, or is this your idea of teasing me mercilessly until I beg for relief?"

A picture popped into my head of Maya arched in the throes of ecstasy on the very ending of climax. The jolt of arousal reached down to the exact spot I was aching for her to touch. I grabbed both her hands in mine and lifted her to a standing position. We both pulled down the covers on the bed and jumped in like two girls at a slumber party. I think I might have been the one to giggle first.

We both turned to face one another at the same time, and almost in unison, reached out to begin our exploration of the other's body.

"We don't have to get creative today, Heaven. I do have various treasures that might add a bit of spice, but today I want to concentrate on you. I want to discover every sensitive spot on each other. There's an awful lot I can do with my fingers…my mouth …my tongue."

Bingo, direct hit to the libido. I was about to tell her that dirty talk might be one thing that we could explore, when she grabbed her head and began shaking uncontrollably.

"It's Leah. Oh, my God, Leah. She's in real trouble. Pain, so much pain."

I soothed her as best I could. "Shhh, tell me what to do. How can I help?" I pulled her into my arms and tried to rub her back, but she kept rocking. I panicked and decided I needed help. I didn't want to leave her curled in a ball on the bed, but I wasn't equipped for this. It broke my heart to see her hands tightly pushed against her head, as she rocked and moaned in the bed. I didn't think I had time to try to soothe her into a different space.

I hurried to put my clothes back on and was happy to see Cleo tentatively approach Maya. Animals have a sixth sense about people, and they know when their human needs them. The fluffy gray cat didn't seem bothered at all by Maya's rocking.

I ran out of the house to get Darla and Syl. *They'll know what to do. They have to. I can't lose Maya now. I've just discovered how much I want to be an us. Forever, an us.*

CHAPTER TWENTY-ONE

There was no way I was going to be polite and knock on the big front door. I burst inside and began yelling for Darla and Syl.

Syl approached first, but Darla wasn't far behind. "Whoa, slow down Heaven, you're gonna give yourself a heart attack."

I was breathing hard, as I tried to get out the words in my panicked state. "Something's wrong with Maya."

I barely noticed the concerned looks of the rest of the Catchers and Weavers as they shuffled into the room. Syl seemed to act as a barrier and motioned for the group to go back in the other direction. She was probably afraid that something truly nasty was going to come out of my subconscious and begin wreaking havoc on the place. I could have told her I was different and had a lot more control over my emotions.

"Syl, can you keep the group occupied while I go see what's going on?" Darla took my arm and began to lead me outside. "Is Maya in Number 15?" she asked in her calm voice.

I nodded vigorously.

"Okay, we're going to go there together and it's going to all be okay. Maya is strong. She's endured far more harrowing situations than a long-range psychic attack."

"A long-range what-the-fuck?" My voice rose at least ten decibels.

Darla just kept prodding me along until we reached the tiny house. She opened the door, took in the scene, and directed me to sit. "Give me a minute, okay?" After she entered the bedroom, she pulled shut the door that separated the bedroom from the rest of the living space.

I was mimicking Maya's rocking, as I began to move back and forth on the couch. A rush of pain and foreboding hit me full on, and I was sure it was coming from Maya. As a matched pair, it seemed likely we would always feel a bit of what the other was experiencing.

I heard quiet murmuring. *Fuck this. I need to see for myself what the hell is happening.* I jumped up and crept closer, putting my ear against the door.

"You have to filter the emotion, separate it from the intel," Darla soothed.

"It hurts, I can't pull it apart."

"Yes, you can. The strainer is right in front of you, and all the emotion is slipping through the holes. Now all you hear is useful information."

I took a step back, turned the knob and slowly opened the door.

Even though Darla had her back to me I heard her sigh. "Well come on in if you must, and make yourself useful."

Maya was still rocking and moaning. I took a step closer and brushed my hand over her head, almost like I was petting a cat. "Maya, can you hear me?"

"Sit on the bed and keep making physical contact. She's experiencing whatever her sister feels at this moment, and it isn't good. I can't seem to get her to separate the feelings from the sights and sounds around her. I think her father is letting Leah project to her sister. He wants them both to feel the pain. Sadistic bastard."

"Should I try? What do I need to do?"

"Are you able to get inside her head at all?"

"Sort of. I connect to her feelings, but words are fuzzy. She's the one who can read my mind and put pictures in my head. I haven't been able to reciprocate yet. Together we projected the norovirus into these guys that were miles away from us, but Maya was the one who led the experiment. Once she put the picture in my head, I was able to help."

"I don't think I can get through to her, but you can. I guess you get a crash course, and we'll have to pray it works. You ready?"

Even though it was distracting to listen to Maya moan, I nodded.

"Okay, first step, you need to connect to her feelings. It won't be pleasant. Once you've done that, I need you to find a way to separate the negative feelings and put them aside. Sometimes it works to imagine stuffing them in a box and locking them inside. I tried to get Maya to put them through a strainer. That's another mental trick. I like kitchen tools, so I'll imagine a gravy separator."

"A tool box with all those neat compartments where you can separate the screws, bolts, nails, hammers, and wrenches?" I offered.

"Sure, if that works for you. Imagine that the thoughts go in one section and the feelings in another. If you can close off the feelings, even better. You're going to have to actively probe Maya, because I think she's using all her energy to keep you from feeling the pain. She won't be happy that I made you go on an archeological dig inside her head. Are you sure you can handle it?"

"Yes, just tell me how to get to those feelings, so I can lock the little fuckers in my red tool box."

"Good, you already have a detailed picture of the toolbox. That's great, Heaven. I hope you're good at metaphorically picking locks. Close your eyes and picture yourself approaching a door with chains wrapped around it. A huge padlock is keeping you from entering the room. And you need to get into that room."

I closed my eyes and imagined that door. It was massive. The steel links were thick and imposing. I hadn't stopped my physical connection with Maya, my hand lightly touching her back. "I see it."

"You've got a lock pick kit in your pocket. Pull it out right now and select one of the picks. You're lucky because you've selected the perfect pick, and when you push it into the large padlock, it pops open on the first try."

I was so excited, because I saw myself as some kind of master thief, able to get into any locked room. "I got it. It's open."

"Pull those chains from the door, and when you open the door, don't let her feelings overwhelm you. They're just on the other side. I can't tell you how they're going to manifest themselves, that's between you and Maya, but be prepared for something big, bad, and ugly."

I took two steps inside, and boy was Darla right. Towering over me was a snarling, face melting, creature, that probably combined all the scariest elements of every single horror movie monster I'd ever seen. His red eyes bore holes into my skull, and I did the first thing that popped into my head. I turned the ugly fucker into a tiny plastic toy and tossed him into my red tool box that had magically appeared. A small silver key materialized in my hand, and I stuck it into the miniature lock, making sure the feelings were confined for now.

I felt like I'd entered some dreamscape, as Maya floated toward me with a radiant smile on her face. There was an almost effervescent yellow glow all around her. She touched my cheek, and there was a sense of peace that surrounded her.

"I knew you'd come. I have information to share." Her voice was quiet and carefully modulated, almost like what she was about to share was no big deal. But I knew different.

I saw myself reach out to her, to make physical contact in this dream world. "You're not in pain anymore?"

"No, thanks to you, but Leah is. We don't have a lot of time. Father is furious and wants his pound of flesh. He doesn't care anymore about keeping her alive. You're the prize he seeks. He's managed to learn that we're a matched pair, so apparently, I've been elevated to someone he wishes to keep alive now."

"How was he able to confirm that?"

"Torture. They're getting ready to put her in the Dream Pod. She won't survive. We have a few hours, because they still believe she has more information to give them. So, her pain will continue. They don't know that Leah has no idea where Darla's center is located. She's my sister. We have to rescue her."

"We will," I confidently answered. I guess being in some kind of living dream allowed me more bravado than when I was in the real world.

"Don't let Syl talk you into waiting to perfect the serum, there isn't time for that."

"I'll volunteer to be her guinea pig, and we'll unleash on them the biggest, baddest, army of monsters I can conjure up."

"We'll do it together. One more thing. Beware of Raven. She has a darkness inside her and is currently teetering on the fence. It won't take much for her to fall to the other side."

Those were her lasts words, as she began to fade until I was left alone in what appeared to be an empty white room.

I opened my eyes and looked at Maya, who wasn't rocking anymore. Her eyes blinked open. "Heaven?"

I stroked her head. "Yeah, baby, I'm right here. God, you scared me."

"I sincerely regret not jumping your bones the very first night I met you."

The absurdity of that comment at such a tense moment caused the laughter to bubble up inside of me. My mirth was contagious, and all three of us fell on the bed in a fit of giggles.

Darla finally raised her eyebrow and said, "I take it you two were interrupted in the midst of a more pleasant activity than probing each other's minds."

"Yeah, something like that," I answered.

Darla turned her attention back to Maya. "I know that Heaven was able to help you separate the feelings from the information. Do you mind providing an update?"

"Timeline is seriously compromised. We need to move now, or Leah won't survive the night," Maya stated.

Darla frowned. "Understood. Okay, I'm going to need both of you to convince Syl to inject all of us. She's a perfectionist, and we don't have the luxury of ensuring precision. I hope she's achieved enough protection to overcome the new enhancements, because if the serum doesn't work, we're royally screwed."

"Um, yeah, I could have done without that dire prediction," I admitted.

"You should know the risks. I can't ask you to attack without knowing all the dangers you might face," Darla said solemnly.

"I'm not letting my sister fight this battle alone."

"And I'm not letting Maya go into the fires of hell by herself," I declared.

"Don't worry, Heaven, none of us will. Come on, it's time to gather the troops."

†

When we entered the main house, Syl met us at the door. She didn't even have to open her mouth; the question hung on her face like a Christmas ornament on a tree.

"Sorry, hon, time has run out for us. We have to move tonight, or Leah and the others might not survive." Darla answered her unasked question. "Are the warriors in the main meeting room?"

Syl nodded. "We've been waiting for you. I'm proud of how they've remained calm. I wish I had more time to prepare everyone and make sure that whatever they throw at us slides off us as if we were made of Teflon."

"It'll have to be enough. Even if Dr. Spartan's new drugs are only partially thwarted, it should provide moderate protection. I'm certain that at fifty percent or more, we'll easily overwhelm them." Darla started walking purposely toward the room where the team had gathered.

Syl fell in step beside her lover. "Oh, I think we'll have at least seventy-five percent fortification over their efforts to shut down the Weavers, who have double the strength with their paired halves helping."

Maya and I followed the couple into the room and found the team sitting in the exact same seats that I'd seen them in when I'd first been introduced to the squad. The seats next to Gretchen and Beanie were open again, and they both grinned at me when I sat down next to the affable couple. Maya settled on the other side of me.

Syl took an empty seat at another table and waited while Darla took her place at the front of the room. I wasn't sure exactly how powerful Darla was, but her leadership abilities were evident in her posture. She had the presence of someone who was supremely confident, and all twenty women waited, giving her the ultimate respect she clearly deserved.

"We've been preparing for this day for a long time. Unfortunately, we don't have the luxury to wait until Syl perfects her serum, but I'm confident it will provide ample protection against their new drugs. Heaven and Maya will take the lead and clear the main path. Each of you will need to spread out and remove any obstacle in your way with whatever means you have." Darla paused, as she made eye contact with each woman in the room. They all seemed to hang on every word. Even Gretchen and Beanie had serious expressions as they listened intently.

Darla took a big breath. "If there is a way to simply contain and control their scientists, lab techs, and handlers without killing them, please choose that avenue. We have one comprehensive goal. Destroy all the technology, drugs, and the whole damn building, but get all the subjects out. Carry those poor souls on your back if you have to, or let your dream manifestations help." Darla looked at me and smiled. "I understand Heaven has a large blue woman who helps, She-Hulk, right?"

I grinned back at her.

"I'll bet she can carry at least one woman. Any chance you can conjure up more than one?"

I shrugged. "I don't know. I can try. Is that something that people can do? You know, create duplicates."

Gretchen bobbed her head up and down. "Beanie and I always pop out a pack of wolves. They're loyal, and it doesn't take a lot of effort to control them, but they sure scare the shit out of anyone they bare their teeth at. Our record is twenty-five." She shifted her massive body and seemed to sit taller in her seat.

"Thanks, Gretchen. I'm glad you provided that example. It helps Heaven know there is no limit to the number of creatures she can dream up," Darla added.

"Good to know," I answered. I'd never popped out more than one monster, but then I'd always felt guilty whenever even one showed up. I hoped Maya would help me change my perspective and think up my army without hesitation.

Maya leaned into me and whispered in my ear, "Piece of cake. You managed to box those projected feelings, that's an advanced skill. Duplication of dream manifestations is child's play."

"Sometimes, I can't help myself when I'm hungry. I conjure up a massive donut that rolls over everything in its path." Gretchen blushed. "Of course, I wouldn't take the chance to eat it after it rolls over the dirt and grime, but when Beanie and me are just practicing, I'm a pretty good baker." Gretchen was so endearing. I didn't know if she'd intended to break the tension, but it worked and I laughed.

"Syl, can you please go draw up the vials of serum for everyone? I'll send them two at a time so we don't overwhelm you in the lab. Gretchen and Beanie, you can head to the lab with Syl right now. When you return, I'll send the next two. Maya and Heaven, I want you two to be the last to receive the serum. If it starts to break down and lose its efficacy, I don't want either of you compromised as our most powerful pair. Unfortunately, you'll be the first in and the last out. Okay?"

Maya nodded and I said, "That works for me."

CHAPTER TWENTY-TWO

As our convoy rolled along, I felt an impending doom and the gooey lump sat heavily in the pit of my stomach. I wasn't like Maya who seemed perfectly poised. I was scared shitless. Everyone else seemed to be hanging their hats on my abilities. *This is nothing compared to the performance anxiety I felt in the shower with Maya. The risk isn't a lackadaisical orgasm. People will get hurt if I can't perform.*

Maya squeezed my hand, as she maneuvered the car along the highway. "Heaven, you can do this. Together we make an unstoppable team. Channel all your anger for what they did to you and Rosie."

"And you," I added. I knew they'd put her through the ringer. It had showed on her face and body and this made me mad.

"For the most part, I'd rather call up other emotions than anger, but I have to be realistic and understand that hate and anger work in these circumstances."

We were coming up on the Dream Center, and Maya increased her speed. I guessed that she wanted to come in hot and leverage any amount of surprise attack she could muster. The guard at the gate barely had time to react. One of my blue She-Hulks appeared out of nowhere. I think she thumped the dude on the head and proceeded to rip open the gate.

With the gate open, our procession moved through and screeched to a stop in front of the massive facility. Maya jumped out and I followed her. Six men shouldered what looked like rifles, aimed, and began firing. I felt a prick and that just pissed me off. I swiped the dart from my shoulder, and six more She-Hulks appeared. After that, the place went crazy. There were wolves, big lizards with arms, winged creatures resembling dragons, something that looked like a cross between Sasquatch and the Abominable Snowman, and other monster-like creatures. I suppose it made sense that the other pairs would conjure up similar creatures to what usually popped out of my dreams, but it was surprising to see the variety.

I wasn't sure what or who manufactured the explosion, until I saw Maya grin at me.

"Did we do that?"

"Sure did," Maya answered.

"How?"

She shrugged, "I guess together we have an explosive personality."

"You're making jokes?" I asked with incredulity.

"Just keep harnessing that anger, Heaven, it's the spark that causes the boom." Maya grabbed my arm and yanked me along. "Come on, time to find Leah and the rest of them."

I looked back over my shoulder and noticed that Gretchen was stumbling. She had several darts sticking out of her arms and legs. The vests Darla provided only protected our torsos. I supposed she didn't move as fast as the others and made for a large target. I wanted to go back and help her, but Maya wouldn't let me. She continued to pull me along.

"If you want to help Gretchen, send her one of your She-Hulks. Have her scoop up Gretchen and take her out of the melee until this is all finished."

I nodded and concentrated on directing one of the big, blue women. Out of the corner of my eye, I saw one of my She-Hulks race to Gretchen, who was now on the ground. Slung over the She-Hulk's shoulder like she was as light as a feather pillow, Gretchen was safely placed in one of the vehicles, out of the center of danger.

I tried not to divert my attention to who else Turnbull's men had hit with those nasty darts, because we needed to get inside quick while we still had somewhat of an advantage.

✝

Once we were inside the building, I noticed that the apparitions appeared to be fighting each other. I wondered if our team didn't have the requisite control needed to focus their monsters.

"How come they're fighting each other?" I asked as we moved along the corridor.

209

"Spartan has some loyal Weavers and Catchers. Mostly men who believe in his philosophy on how to create the perfect soldiers for war. He's been grooming them for quite some time. He found out early in his experiments that paired women were more powerful. Emotion fuels the apparitions to a greater degree. After that little revelation, he focused on nabbing young girls to develop his army." Maya provided all this information as we ran down the hall. Her voice came out in fits and starts, as she began to breathe more heavily. I wondered about the three darts she'd brushed away from her body and if somehow, they were affecting her ability to move through the complex. I'd been lucky, since only one dart seemed to hit its mark.

Maya pushed open a door to a large room. The look of surprise on Dr. Spartan's face was priceless. He was in the middle of connecting the wires coming from Leah's body. Dr. Spartan made the last connection and flipped a switch on the complicated machine to the right of the chair that Leah remained restrained to. "Leah, I order you to contain the intruders. Use everything at your disposal."

Six snarling, drooling, red-eyed creatures appeared in the compact room and morphed the air into a putrid green mist, as they breathed in and out of their foul noses and mouths. Instead of carbon dioxide, I imagined the monsters were breathing in the oxygen and expelling their own toxic chemical.

I coughed a few times and looked to Maya for direction.

"Gas masks," she shouted.

Thinking things up on the fly wasn't my strong suit, but I had perfected the ability to take direction well. A second later, both Maya and I were sporting funky gas masks that looked a lot like World War II gear. They weren't exactly a fashion statement but seemed to work just fine.

"Leah too," Maya amended. Whoops, I'd forgotten to give Leah her own fashion accessory. I modified my error quickly.

The foul air wasn't our only problem. The disgusting creatures took a few steps forward to theoretically rip us to shreds. I didn't wait for instruction. The room became overcrowded with my own version of creatures from a dark lagoon. I hadn't noticed Dr. Spartan fleeing the compact space, as the two groups of dream manifestations began to battle each other. Snarling mouths and razor-sharp claws locked together in an impressive show of strength. I felt like I was watching six Japanese *Godzilla vs. Mothra* movies playing side by side.

There wasn't enough space in the small room for us and the apparitions. Maya ripped off the wires connected to the now-destroyed machine. The restraints proved more challenging, so I conjured up my go-to protector, She-Hulk, and the big blue woman made quick work of the flimsy manacles. I assumed the other six She-Hulks were continuing to battle in other parts of the complex.

She-Hulk number seven tossed Leah over her shoulder at the same time Maya grabbed my hand and pulled me from the overcrowded room, leaving the monsters to duke it out on their own. If Leah's creations were anything like mine, they would disappear on their own after about thirty minutes.

Leah was flopping around like a rag doll on She-Hulk's shoulder, as we all ran from the room. We stopped for a second in the corridor and pulled off the masks. The putrid green air hadn't seeped from the room we'd just vacated. I took two deep breaths and saw Maya do the same.

Maya pulled off Leah's mask and placed her fingers against Leah's throat. "I don't know what they did to her, but her pulse, while a bit erratic, seems strong. I think we need to remove her from the chaos."

"She-Hulk, please take her to one of the cars," I directed.

In a flash, my favorite protector was gone, running through the crumbling building and managing to avoid the debris as she headed outside. Although there was some fighting at the end of the corridor, our immediate vicinity was clear. We took a momentary breather to gather our wits.

We moved more slowly down the corridor, pushing open doors, only to find several empty rooms. When we had almost reached a skirmish that was producing high-pitched screams and other otherworldly sounds. I tried the doorknob. The damn thing was locked, so I knew there was something important behind door number one.

I barely had to think when another She-Hulk materialized and smashed her body against the locked door. The splinters of wood flew everywhere, and we entered the cavernous room. Dormitory-style twin beds stood in neat rows, at least fifty of them. I brought my hand over my mouth in an attempt to stem my nausea, as I looked at the young girls chained to the beds. Their panicked eyes met mine. Most of them looked emaciated, and all of them wore the pained expression I knew so well from my time in the center. Their pale faces and haunted eyes pleaded for release.

I didn't even have to ask She-Hulk to start on their chains. The look on her faced showed her humanity, and I wondered how a dream apparition could reveal so much emotion.

Maya looked at me with concern. "We're going to need a bus or two, and an army of something that will gather these girls. Can you do that? I'll help."

I nodded. I felt a flood of love and compassion, and that's when I realized that while anger and hate fueled the double-barreled monsters battling outside, the opposite emotions would enable Maya and I to generate exactly what was needed to save those kids.

I felt the energy drain from me, as forty-nine more She-Hulks materialized and began methodically busting the chains from the captive girls.

I was surprised when Raven burst into the room. At first her hard expression seemed impenetrable. She opened her mouth as if to say something, then must have registered the unfolding scene. Her expression softened as she looked at the pitiful girls moving slowly after being released from their chains.

With a gentleness I didn't know my She-Hulks possessed, they gathered their charges in their arms and began walking them out of the room. I prayed that none of them would run into difficulty before they made it to the three buses.

I guess all that conjuring I wasn't even giving a second thought to had depleted my energy. I collapsed on the floor. I remember looking into Maya's loving gaze, as she gathered me in her arms.

"Make a decision, Raven. Which side will you align with?" I heard Maya ask.

I looked up and stared into Raven's eyes and saw the look of resolve. I lost consciousness without knowing which team she would choose.

†

When I came to a few minutes later, Maya was on one side and Raven on the other. They practically carried me out of the building. Darla met us on the way out and frowned.

"What happened?" Darla asked.

"We can't be the last ones out anymore. She's used up everything she has. I'm sorry, I can't help any longer. I'm on my last reserves as well," Maya answered.

Darla nodded. "I think we're winning. We'll take it from here, just get her out. Raven, I'm glad to see the choice you've made. I know you can do it, continue to fight the pull."

Raven had a grim expression but nodded. It looked like something was draining her energy too.

"They got to Leah as well. We'll have to watch her closely. I'd hate to chemically restrain her after all she's been through…" Maya let the words dangle.

"It's okay. I have faith in Syl's abilities," Darla answered.

"So do I," Maya answered.

They were talking in code, a covert conversation that only they seemed to understand. Maybe Raven also, as she flinched when Darla mentioned chemical restraints and Syl's abilities. It didn't matter, because I was done. Flipped over on the grill and perfectly crispy.

"Go now, we'll meet you back at the house. Get some rest, because tonight we will celebrate our victory." Darla smiled.

"I love your confidence." Maya returned her grin.

Before my noodle body flopped into the passenger seat of Maya's car, I heard several loud explosions. *I suppose I'm not the only one with an explosive personality.* I chuckled at the joke I made inside my head.

Maya gave me a strange look, but I just smiled back at her. Either she'd read my mind, or I would tell her all about it later, after I had a chance to grow back my skeleton. I hoped she would be proud of the fact that I was starting to lighten up. Maybe this was the step on my journey to take life less seriously and enthusiastically join Maya in her adventures.

CHAPTER TWENTY-THREE

The ride back to the Dream Seekers' Commune was relatively uneventful. I wanted to help get all the girls settled, but Maya staunchly refused. I suppose the fact that I wasn't very stable when I emerged from the car didn't help. Raven stepped up to the plate, and I think she was in her element as she began ordering around the cloned She-Hulks, who carried the girls from the buses.

Maya had whispered something in Raven's ear, and I wondered where in the world they were going to put everyone. They didn't need rooms for my She-Hulks because they were due to dissipate soon. I suspected Maya was giving them a boost until they completed their mission to make sure all the girls were settled inside.

It worried me that I hadn't seen Jimena. I wondered if Dr. Spartan had used her as leverage. *Is that why Raven was on the fence? If they had Maya, I'd do almost anything to save her, so who am I to judge?*

Some of the girls didn't look so good. I hoped Syl would be back soon to check them out. A few might need medical attention beyond food, water, and a comfortable bed. Before we went to our tiny house, I asked, "Where will they take them?"

"There's a makeshift medical facility behind the house and another large dormitory that should provide their basic needs until we can figure out what to do with them. Some might have families they can go back to, who probably don't have any idea what was happening. Other kids could be on their own and honestly, I don't have any clue how we'll approach that challenge."

I didn't want to add to her concern, but I thought she should get a dose of reality. "Maya, even the kids with families might not have a bright future with their loved ones."

"I know. Sometimes it's not enough to have a parent who loves you. My mother tried. It's what caused her demise. I don't know what happened to Leah's mother, but mine was exterminated without hesitation. When she found out what my father was doing with me, she tried to take me away. My tactics were very different from Leah's. I let him believe my usefulness was extremely limited. Leah used her skill, talents that he grossly underestimated. If anyone has reason to hate my father, it's me, but I won't let hate take over my whole sense of being."

"I'm glad you're not like Leah."

"I do regret not showing the depths of my gifts when I had the chance to save my mother. I'd decided to show my hand, but by then it was too late. Leah picks at that wound every time I disagree with her, and I must admit her narrow attack hits its mark every time. But, I will never share my half-sister's single-minded purpose to destroy our father. At least you had normal parents."

I recognized Maya's need to change the focus from her childhood and readily offered up my own pain. I wanted to take away her discomfort any way I could. I was pleased she had opened up as much as she had.

"My parents had no clue what to do with me, and they were looking for an easy out. If someone had knocked on my folks' door with the intent to deliver me back to their care, I don't believe they would have welcomed me with open arms." I worried about the fate of the girls.

Maya frowned. "Damn, we need a better system to deal with kids who struggle."

I nodded my agreement.

I was glad when we finally made it to the door of our little house. My legs were quite wobbly as I stumbled inside. Maya helped me to the bed, and I succumbed to my exhaustion as I laid down.

Although I was anxious to hear about the results of our assault, I let myself relax. I remained awake, as Maya curled her fingers into my hair. There is nothing more relaxing than when someone plays with your hair. I should have been more wound up, but the combination of exhaustion and her magic fingers calmed me down so much, I wasn't pacing like I normally would have.

"You can continue to keep doing that for, oh, how about an eternity?" I joked.

Maya chuckled. "How are you feeling?"

"Like I'm just getting over a particularly nasty bout of pneumonia. Totally devoid of energy."

"Hmmm, I take it that you have personal experience with that illness."

"Yeah, I think they were actually scared I might die when I got double pneumonia in Spartan's lab. I suppose that's what you get when mistreating the lab rats." My body was trashed, but my mind was racing.

"I never did understand how my father thought he would gain loyalty from those he enslaved."

"Exactly. It's like the terrible conditions in China or Africa. Did you know that all the chocolate we consume comes off the backs of ten thousand boys and girls who are abducted from the west coast of Africa? When I learned that, I never ate another piece of chocolate again, unless I knew exactly where it had come from. The big chocolate producers signed an agreement to end the worst of the child labor abuses, but it hasn't stopped, and everyone is still eating cheap chocolate. It is a multi-billion-dollar industry. The cocoa farmers abduct them, enslave them, make them work twelve hours a day, beat them, and starve them. Some of the kids are as young as seven. It's deplorable, and the chocolate industry knows all about it." I shook my head. Child slavery was a topic I was passionate about.

"Something about that formula must work, otherwise those harsh tactics wouldn't continue. They almost turned Raven, and I'm not sure how Leah was affected," Maya said sadly.

"Yeah, but I think there is more to it. Dr. Spartan uses a combination of torture, drugs, and I don't even want to venture a guess at what that machine he had Leah hooked up to was doing." I yawned. "Please don't let me fall asleep. I'm worried about all the rest of the team who had to stay back and finish the siege. I don't think I could live with the guilt if even one of them is seriously hurt."

"Shhh. I have the utmost faith. Besides, from what I saw, we were totally kicking their asses. You did an amazing job, Heaven. I've never seen a Weaver bring to life so many protectors."

"I'm pretty sure you were right there with me, amplifying everyone."

Maya smiled. "Maybe I helped a little bit."

Despite my best efforts, my eyelids felt so heavy that I finally surrendered to sleep.

✝

I woke up to a commotion outside the bedroom window. I popped up ready to join the team, because the short nap did a world of good for my energy level.

Maya stretched and yawned. "It sounds like we'll get to find out how things went."

"God, you are the most Zen person I've ever met. How can you be so relaxed?" I glanced back at Maya. I'd already made it to the door by the time her feet hit the ground.

She shrugged and swiveled as she climbed out of bed. I opened the door. I didn't see any fatal wounds on the women piling out of the cars and heading to the main house. Darla wasn't exactly smiling, but she wasn't frowning either. A few of the women, including Beanie, looked a little disheveled and were limping. Syl was holding a large piece of gauze against her shoulder.

I burst into the parade of women. "Is everyone okay? Did we manage to destroy that heinous place?"

Darla turned to look at me. "We have a few people who need medical attention, but all in all, we came away from the mission relatively unscathed. Can you and Maya go find Gretchen? We'll debrief in the large meeting room."

Maya had silently joined me and took my hand. "I told Raven to settle Gretchen in her house. Come on, we'll see how she's doing. Hopefully the effect of the darts has worn off by now. Syl's serum should have reduced their potency."

†

Gretchen staggered a little on the way to the conference room, where we joined the rest of the Dream Warriors. It seemed like everyone had assigned seating, as we took the same spots at the table where we'd previously staked out our territory. Beanie smiled at Gretchen. I noticed how groggy Gretchen seemed. Her eyes were rapidly fluttering, as if she wanted to blink away her confusion. She sat heavily, and Beanie kissed her on the cheek.

"Hello, Love," Beanie whispered.

Raven sat at an adjacent table, with her hands clasped in front of her. Her eyes kept shifting around the room, and I wondered if she was hoping to see Jimena, but I couldn't find her anywhere either. I did see a bedraggled Deidre, with Francine, Brenda, and Star. That answered my question regarding whether Brenda and Star were on our side or Dr. Spartan's.

I suspect Raven couldn't wait for Darla to address the room; her voice quivered as she asked, "Jimena?"

"Her wounds were…" Darla began.

"No, no, no." Raven bowed her head and began to sob.

"You didn't let me finish. We are not equipped to care for her injuries here. She was admitted to Good Samaritan. She's in serious condition, but she'll make it."

Raven jumped up. "A car, I need a car."

Darla nodded, and Syl tossed her a set of keys. "It's the red SUV just outside."

Darla grabbed her arm. "Sorry, Raven. Before you leave, Syl has to give you an injection. You understand, right? We can't take a chance."

Raven nodded. "Fine, but can we hurry please?"

"Follow me, it will only take a minute or two. It's not fail-safe, but if he didn't get a chance to hook you up, it'll work well," Syl said.

"He didn't. Leah was going to be his first," Raven answered.

"You'll still need to spend time with one of our team after you return. I'll expect you to work with one of our Catchers as soon as you get back, if you plan to stay with us," Darla stated.

Raven nodded and followed Syl, as they both headed for the door.

"Syl," Darla called out. "While you're giving Raven that injection, you need to have that shoulder attended to. I'll be in there in a few minutes to help after we debrief."

"I'll expect everyone else with even a tiny scratch to go to the medical facility after you're done," Syl answered before leaving the room with Raven in tow.

I wasn't sure what that bit about the injection was all about. Leah was conspicuously absent from the gathering.

Maya frowned, and that was such a rare thing. *Whatever that interchange meant, it isn't good.* "What the hell was that all about?" I whispered in Maya's ear.

"Later," she answered.

"I'm not going to keep you all here for very long, because you need rest and most of you could use a little first aid. Besides, you heard Syl, she expects to see many of your lovely faces shortly. She's definitely not someone to cross. I tend to want to stay on her good side." There was a murmuring in the group and a few chuckles.

Darla continued, "There are a few members of the Dream Warriors who need an update, and there's something else I want everyone to think about." Darla paused and took a big breath. "Gerald Turnbull and Dr. Spartan managed to escape. Although we did destroy their facility, and their warriors are in chaos right now without someone to direct them, I don't think they'll give up."

"They won't. Cash flow for their program is endless. The government wants this badly and will help them establish a new center in a different location. Living nightmares projected from a safe distance are something that is damn near impossible to fight against. If you want to end this thing, you're going to have to find a way to stop Dr. Spartan and my father." Maya paused and smiled. "I have an idea. Perhaps a little reverse engineering. What's good for the goose is good for the gander. Heaven's already demonstrated her ability to roam around inside a person's head and lock away negative feelings. Together, I think we could turn the tables for good."

"Hmmm. Maybe you have something there, but you wanted the assistance. You needed help. I don't see either your father or Spartan being very receptive." Darla leaned on the table, and I noticed how drawn her face looked.

"We'll do it together. In just a few weeks, she's gone from conjuring uncontrollable creatures during sleep, to delivering multiple protectors while fully awake. Her skill is far greater than I thought, even without my amplification." Maya looked at me, and I could tell she wanted me to agree.

"I don't know what I'm doing, but count me in," I offered.

"Syl injected Leah, right?" Maya asked.

Darla nodded. "She also gave her a sedative that will keep her subdued for the night."

"Someone needs to watch her closely. She's compromised and powerful," Maya warned.

"I'm well aware of that." Darla turned her focus back on the group. "Everyone needs to be on high alert."

"What about the girls we rescued? What's going to happen to them?" I asked.

Darla sighed. "One problem at a time. For now, we'll have to keep them here."

"Syl can't take care of everyone," I protested.

Maya stroked my arm. "She has help, don't worry. The facility has other doctors who help out."

I raised my eyebrow. "How come you guys eek out information in tiny bits and pieces?"

Maya chuckled. "I didn't know the fact that we have other medical professionals was some big secret." She shrugged. "I guess it never came up."

"How big is this place?" I asked.

"Big enough," Maya and Darla said together.

"Damn cryptic women," I mumbled.

"Okay everyone, go get some rest and make sure you're patched up. Anyone who wants to volunteer to spend time with the girls to give them some reassurance, except Heaven or Maya, follow Beanie."

"How come we can't volunteer to spend time with the kids?" I whispered to Maya.

She smiled. "Because I have plans for you."

CHAPTER TWENTY-FOUR

I had a lot of questions about Leah and Raven. It seemed like there was no end to what Dr. Spartan and Turnbull would do to test people's boundaries. *I have the distinct impression that Maya, Darla, and Syl know exactly what those two are capable of. Maya doesn't seem to trust Leah, and something Spartan did has amplified her suspicion.*

We walked hand in hand back to our little place. I was becoming increasingly comfortable with the idea of living with Maya in our snug little house and hoped that option was on the table. I suppose we still had loose ends to take care of, but it was a nice thought. *Does it depend on me being able to do what Maya suggested?*

I put that beast of negative emotions in the red tool box as a lark. Darla directed me every step of the way. What would happen if the nasty little bugger managed to escape and join forces with whatever dark matter hung out in Spartan and Turnbull's brains? What if that crap completely took over my thoughts and feelings? Before Maya, I was definitely prone to swings where the deep pit was all I could see. *Is she somehow helping me compartmentalize my feelings and allowing me to shove the depression into a locked container, without me even knowing she's doing it? Sure, I have some Catcher abilities, but my dominant skill is as a Weaver.*

I wondered what plans Maya had for me, as she led me into the bedroom. We'd had a short nap before everyone returned, but it wasn't like we'd managed to restore all our depleted energy. Too many times we'd been interrupted, and I wasn't sure I wanted to start anything when we were all supposed to be on high alert.

"Um, Maya, not that I—"

Maya laughed. "Oh Heaven, you are so precious. My plans are to spoil you rotten by giving you a head rub and allowing you to return to full capacity. It'll kind of be like topping off your gas tank so that you are completely full and ready for an impromptu road trip."

"Oh." I was a little disappointed, even though I understood and didn't disagree.

I heard what sounded like scratching on the front door and turned to Maya. She cocked her head and listened, then smiled as she went to open the door.

Satan ran inside and jumped on the bed. He acted like he owned the place.

I laughed. "I wonder if the little bugger smelled me or something."

Maya flopped on the bed, gently pushed Satan to the bottom, and kicked off her shoes. "Come on, join me and let me take you to nirvana. I promise I give the best head rubs." She sat against the headboard looking expectantly at me.

She didn't have to ask me twice. I jumped next to her, skootched down, and laid my head on her lap. She was looking down at me with such an expression of love, I was putty in her hands. "Why don't you tell me what all that talk about Raven and Leah was about? How come Syl had to give them injections?"

Maya started moving her fingers through my hair and gently rubbing my scalp. "Brenda and Star have been collaborating with us. Brenda is particularly skilled at obtaining information."

I saw Satan inch closer to me until he curled up on my other side with a paw draped possessively over the center of my body.

"I'll just bet she is. I guess if you're going to have a double agent, a sex addict might be useful on our team."

Maya chuckled. "Brenda's okay. She has her moments and was able to confirm what we had suspected. Dr. Spartan was working on a new drug that, when used in conjunction with that machine you saw Leah hooked up to, has the ability to control his army of Weavers and Catchers. Syl was a few steps ahead of him and started working on a serum to neutralize the effects. Unfortunately, the machine is new, and we don't know the full effects of that technology."

Her hands were magic and I started to become drowsy. "That's sounds dangerous."

"We've got it under control."

I wanted to stay awake and ask more questions, but I eventually succumbed to the relaxation of the head rub and Satan's loud purring. I must have fallen asleep.

†

I was having a wonderful dream where I was in the throes of passion with Maya. She was doing some very inventive things with her tongue. Someone shook my shoulders, and I wondered if, in my state of pleasure, I'd inadvertently conjured up another exotic dancer.

My eyes blinked open, and the look on Maya's face shook me from the incoherence of deep sleep.

"It's coming, Heaven. Time to wake up. They've found us. Leah brought them here. I should have known. I've put us all at risk. I guess everything does happen in threes. I was bound to have a third major regret."

"What are you talking—"

Leah burst into the house, and she had a crazed look in her eyes. She reminded me of Medusa. Her hair wasn't quite made of snakes, yet it looked alive. It was creepy.

"You were supposed to be my yin, not Maya's. Father promised." Leah pointed her finger at Maya. "You were supposed to die. This is all your fault, and now you and your band of misfits will get exactly what you deserve. I will find another match. You disgust me," Leah snarled.

Maya was calm as she stood. "Leah, they've implanted false thoughts and memories into your head. You've got to fight it. It isn't your fault."

Leah placed her hands against her head and moaned. "You're lying. He warned me about that." She turned her attention to me with an icy glare.

"Heaven, use a shield." Maya whispered to me.

I looked at her like she had two heads. I didn't have the foggiest idea what she was talking about. I started to feel that tickle in my head, and I knew that Leah was starting her invasion. "Oh, got it." I slammed my eyes shut and envisioned a steel dome protecting both Maya and myself.

"Argh. You don't matter anymore, I don't need either of you." Leah growled and fled the house, her hair flowing wildly. For a second, I thought it had turned into live snakes.

"Holy shit, what was that all about?"

"No time to explain. We've got to join the team. Dear old Dad hung his hat on turning the wrong daughter. I think he believes that Leah is the more powerful one. I guess maintaining a low profile works." Maya grinned. "This is going to be fun."

"Are you nuts?"

"Of course, we are all a little nuts, otherwise he never would have experimented on us. Come on baby, let's have another adventure together."

†

When Turnbull and Spartan's army advanced on our compound, they didn't have any rifles with darts, only their male Weavers and Catchers. Leah appeared to be leading the attack. I almost felt sorry for her; it was such a lopsided battle. Our Catchers kept turning their creatures into kittens or puppies. Sometimes, the lizard-like monsters became geckos or tree frogs. When our Dream Warriors couldn't think of what to turn the monsters into, they became plastic toys.

I had to fight myself from laughing or losing interest in the fight. But Maya didn't even bother to temper her mirth, as we made our way through everything they lobbed at us.

I think Turnbull sincerely thought he would have the upper hand. He knew he'd managed to turn his daughter, who was supposed to be the virus, infecting the rest of us. When we came face to face with him and Dr. Spartan, I wasn't sure if it was only my rage or the collective rage of all the Dream Warriors. What we managed to bring forth was truly the most horrifying creature I'd ever witnessed.

In less than thirty seconds, an amalgamation of every single horror movie creature I'd ever seen ripped apart both Dr. Spartan and Maya's father. The beast shook its hairy, scaly head and roared, shooting an impressive amount of fire into the air. It was the most gruesome scene I'd ever witnessed. I wasn't sure I'd ever be able to shake that vision from my mind, and I worried about the nightmares I would have about this day. I wanted the destruction to stop. I couldn't bear to see anyone else experience the same fate.

"Stop. Enough," I shouted. "No more, no more."

The men and Leah dropped to their knees, holding their heads in their hands and wailing.

The collective monster dissipated, until it was no longer in our real world.

"Go to them. Try to remove their dark thoughts," Darla directed. "If you aren't strong enough to remove the destructive cloud, don't attempt it. I don't want anyone turning inside themselves and taking on the gloom."

I dropped to my knees, and the guilt I felt threatened to send me into that dark tunnel, never to return to the light. I was sobbing with the knowledge that, once again, one of my monsters had committed murder. "What have I done? What have I done?" I wailed.

Maya bent next to me, and I felt her soothing energy weave its way in. "Oh, honey, that was not just your monster. The collective anger of so many brought the dream alive. There wasn't anything you could have done to prevent this. I know this is not what you wanted to happen, but please, don't leave me for that dark place. I don't think I would recover from that."

My tear-stained face looked up at my other half. I believe that seeing her love and concern was the only thing that prevented me from spiraling into forever darkness. I couldn't let history repeat itself. If I lost Maya, my yang, I would turn those monsters back to me. I would direct them to rip me to shreds. I didn't want Maya to feel the loss that I'd experienced.

"Yes, baby, come back to me. Forgive yourself, and we can move on together."

Together. That sounded good to me, and I forced that horrific nightmare from my head. Willing it to never return.

The matched pairs descended on the army of men. They would do what I had done when Maya was in so much pain. No one was approaching Leah, as she rocked back and forth on her heels, seeming to experience the worst of whatever had afflicted Turnbull's army. Her anguish would be the most difficult to contain. I looked at Maya for her agreement that she and I needed to be the ones to try.

She nodded.

I was getting comfortable with my pal, She-Hulk, and thought that she might be able to help us out one more time. I would miss my big blue protector when I no longer had need for her services. It wasn't like we ever had riveting discussions about contemporary politics, but still, she'd been instrumental in getting me out of a few tight spots.

I didn't want to try to move Leah myself; I wasn't sure how she might react. She-Hulk appeared and immediately went to where Leah was locked inside some kind of hell. I expected Leah to fight back, but she simply let She-Hulk pick her up. Maya and I followed the two of them into our tiny residence.

†

I'd traveled to the depths of depression before, so I had a small inkling about what Leah might be experiencing. No matter how much of a cold-hearted bitch she'd shown herself to be, it was heartbreaking to watch her in that state of mental incapacity.

After She-Hulk had dumped her on the couch, Leah immediately pulled herself into a human ball and began rocking again. Her wailing penetrated every corner of the small space, and it was hard to hear myself think, much less listen to Maya's instruction.

"Heaven, you have to go inside her head and locate the darkness. I'll give you my strength and guide you. Whatever method you choose to separate that manufactured gloom is up to you, but once you have that surgically removed from Leah's normal emotions, you have to put it somewhere where it won't escape."

"I like my red toolbox."

"You need to be especially careful, because the darkness is almost like an entity of its own, seeking out a nice cozy place to reside. Your mind is the logical location to move to, because you'll be right there for the damn thing to hop into, especially with those raw self-deprecating emotions you've just experienced."

Maya was giving me new strength.

"Got it. Lock it away before it takes up residence in my head. I'm ready."

I always had to shut my eyes to concentrate. My confidence was immediately bolstered, when I saw Maya standing beside me as we began to walk, hand in hand, through this thick green fog. I liked the color green, but this was beyond creepy. After we made it to the other side, we came face to face with what we needed to lock away. This time there wasn't a need to unlock a door. I wondered why but abandoned that thought, because we were on a mission.

Geez, do these negative feelings always have to manifest themselves as a snarling, face melting, creature? This thing could be a sibling of the monster I encountered in Maya. I'll lock this fucker away too. Is that thing smiling?

This being seemed twice the size of the last, and there seemed to be a look of joy on the beast's face. I don't know exactly what happened next, but I found myself in a brick circle, and Maya was no longer beside me. The space was small and dark. It felt like I was in a well. The air around me was dank and putrid, and I didn't want to breathe in the foul molecules.

I barely heard an echo of Maya's voice, so far away that I scarcely heard her.

"Heaven, stay with me, don't go there. Fight it."

I sat on the dirt floor and pulled my legs up against my chest. This was a place I was familiar with. I was so tired. I saw the creature I'd had a role in, who had ripped apart Turnbull and Spartan. The scene began playing again and again in an infinite loop. Tired of fighting. Tired of feeling the dramatic ups and downs that my illness dictated. It didn't matter that since I'd met Maya, I hadn't felt the same. Sure, I hadn't experienced those intense mood swings lately, but deep down I knew they would return. Yes, it was easier to stay in this hole. It was where I deserved to be.

The echo of Maya's voice appeared to come closer, as she said, "Please, Heaven. I need you. I love you. Find the light. Follow the light back to me and together with love, we will send that darkness away."

A tiny prick of light appeared in front of me, and the well was no longer a circular room but a kind of maze. The white dot danced in front of me, and I was reminded of the laser light Maya and I had conjured up for Cleo. I felt a small burst of energy and a desire to follow the bouncing light. So I stood and took a step forward. And then another. Soon, I was seeing a faint light.

I squinted my eyes and could barely make out the fuzzy edges of a person, probably a woman. As I kept putting one foot in front of the other, the person at the edge of the tunnel opening started to gain clarity. Maya stood there with her arms outstretched.

I could feel a heavy breath on my neck and smelled the foul odor. Before I turned around to see what was behind me, Maya's voice rang clear.

"Don't turn around. It can't take over unless you let it or acknowledge it."

I began to gag as the putrid odor invaded my nostrils. Maya jerked her head to the right, and then I noticed my red toolbox.

"Together. We'll do this together. The power of love will always prevail."

I was afraid, but I took another step closer and avoided the temptation to look over my shoulder. I could do this. *Maya is depending on me, and I love her. It's so clear to me now.* "Yes, love," I said out loud.

Maya smiled, and I took that last step into her arms. I whispered in her ear. "I love you too."

The dark tunnel transformed into bright sunshine and a meadow of wildflowers. I looked up at the pale, azure sky with wispy clouds lazily drifting in slow motion. My body felt light, and I wanted to reach up and touch one of the white striations. At that moment, I think Maya could have convinced me to jump out of a plane with her. I believed I was invincible.

When I brought my head down and looked into Maya's loving emerald eyes, she smiled and pointed at my red tool box. There was a solid, steel chain wrapped around the box several times, closed with a ginormous padlock. Maya had an old-fashioned skeleton key in her hand that was an exaggerated size, and I grinned when she wiggled it in the air.

"All locked up. No way is that vile funnel of evil getting out now. Good job, Heaven."

I wasn't sure I was the one to put the final touches on jailing the nasty fucker, but I was happy to hear the task had been completed.

Like a magic trick, everything dispersed in this dream world I found myself in. All that remained was the beautiful meadow and Maya holding her hand out to me. I chuckled to myself, the dream world's version of riding off into the sunset in a happily ever after ending. I knew this wasn't the end but really just the beginning, and I was looking forward to finally having Maya all to myself without interruption. She'd insinuated that when we did finally make love it would be epic, and I was going to hold her to that promise.

CHAPTER TWENTY-FIVE

In the distance, I heard Maya calling my name. I didn't want to come out of this wonderful dream I was having. Maya was by my side as we walked along. My little buck came out to greet us and let me pet his cold, black nose. His pink tongue snaked out to lick my hand and I giggled.

I heard my name again and this time it sounded desperate, so I let my eyes pop open. I found that same color of green from the meadow when I looked into Maya's concerned eyes. My smile must have tempered her worry, because her expression transformed and she pressed her lips on mine. She gathered me in her arms, crushing me against her body.

"Breathe, um, Maya, I need to breathe to continue living," I squeaked.

She immediately released her tight hold and separated from me, while still maintaining some physical contact. Her hands held onto my sides lightly. "We thought we'd lost you to the dream abyss. Sometimes that happens when dark thoughts take over. It's why some mental health patients seem to fold inside themselves and never rejoin the real world. A few of our sisters have gone there, and we weren't able to save them." Maya looked away.

I brushed my hand against her cheek. "You pulled me out. You told me you loved me. Is that only true in my dream world, because if it is, I want to go back."

"Most definitely not, so you'd better not. I have plans for you." She grinned as she started to weave her hand under my shirt. Tugging at the bottom, she asked, "May I?"

I nodded with such vigor, I thought I would give myself whiplash.

She pulled the shirt over my head as she caressed my sides in a touch so light, I barely registered it, but it sent goosebumps up and down my body nevertheless. I wondered if I would survive what I guessed would be an Olympic performance in teasing.

"You are one hundred percent correct, Heaven. I am going to tease you until you beg me for release."

"Oh, God," I groaned, as she gently pushed me on my back, while deftly undoing my bra and slipping it off. The tips of her fingers traveled down to my navel, where she made a small circle twice around the edge, before her index finger continued to the top of my jeans.

I was already squirming when she popped the top button, and I felt her pulling on the zipper. I wasn't sure how she was able to barely touch the edge of where I was most sensitive as she undid the zipper. That tiny trick had me bucking to get her to rub against that spot again. Maya just shook her head.

Her hands moved to the sides of my ass, where a gentle squeeze was all it took. I obediently lifted my butt, so that it was easier for her to pull down my pants. I blushed when she stared. The blue thong wasn't my normal choice for underwear, but when I'd found the stash in the bedside drawer, I thought, *Why not be adventurous for once in my life?*

Once again, her fingers journeyed back and forth across my neatly trimmed triangle of hair that was currently covered by the flimsy undergarment. It felt like she was reading braille on my body and taking the time to understand the full meaning of the words. I was dying for her to rip off my undies and plunge her finger into the depth of my wetness.

"Patience, my love, we'll get there."

I didn't bother trying to block her from grabbing my thoughts, because sharing added to the intimacy of the moment. I loved knowing that she could perfectly read every single reflection and reaction to what she was doing to me.

She hooked a finger on the string of the thong, carefully tugging each side as she maneuvered the last barrier to my throbbing center. She was so excruciatingly slow to remove this piece of clothing that I groaned in frustration and tried to position my body in a way that made it easy for her to touch where I needed her most.

"Nuh uh, Heaven, or I won't take you to the promised land."

"You know, Maya, that is a very sacrilegious thing to say."

She chuckled. "So, shall I stop right now then?"

"Mean, you are just mean."

"I take it that being a heretic might be okay then?"

"Please, Maya." I was definitely not above begging, since I was ready to burst at the slightest touch to my center.

Maya smiled and adopted her serene look. My underwear was discarded without fanfare. I looked at the pile of my clothes clumped together on the floor. *At least they won't feel lonely huddled together.*

I don't think Maya liked me having random thoughts that weren't connected to how good she was making me feel. She traced her finger up the inside of my leg, and I snapped to attention.

We were back to braille again. *For fuck's sake! Is she reading War and Peace on the inside of my thigh? And, oh God, my...* All internal thoughts fled from my mind, when a finger lightly brushed my clit. I gasped. "Back to that spot, please."

"Mmmm this hair is the same lovely golden hue. Beautiful."

Maya pushed open my legs, used her fingers to separate the outer lips, and soon I felt the glorious sensation of the tip of her tongue on my swollen bundle of nerves. I wasn't sure how she'd managed to position herself so quickly between my legs. As her tongue and mouth made love to me, my arousal pushed further and further to the sky. I was flying as I reached heights I'd never been to. The ascent was unhurried and deliberate, building and building.

Maya took a brief second to command me, "Come for me, Heaven."

"I'm so close," I managed to answer, as I hovered on the precipice.

I felt her return to my center, and I tumbled over in an odd combination of a mellow and fiery climax. It's hard to describe how the two opposite sensations would come together like that, but I don't know how else to describe it. The intensity was epic, and yet the peace that accompanied the glorious feeling made it something unique and special.

I settled back against the bed, still feeling the tiny pulses of an orgasm that seemed to extend well beyond the normal time that it usually took for the feelings to subside. "Okay, I definitely just took a journey to the promised land, so you can be blasphemous any time you want. I love you too, by the way, and not because you just delivered me to nirvana."

"I know. I could feel the emotion pulse all around you." Maya crawled up my body and kissed me with the same combination of gentleness and sizzle. I could taste the flavor of my arousal on her lips, and somehow that didn't feel weird or icky to me. It was strangely erotic. I wanted to quickly divest Maya of her clothes and experience her unique essence, but I needed a few minutes. I loved the feel of her body covering mine, but my desire to feel skin on skin triumphed over my need to replenish my energies.

I flipped Maya over and growled. "My turn." I proceeded to remove her clothes, probably not as sensually as she'd managed to do with me, but my technique got the job done. I used the few tricks I had up my own sleeves to deliver her to paradise. Her sigh at the end of our lovemaking was music to my ears. Yes, she was, without a shadow of a doubt, my yang. I would cherish her until my soul left this plane of existence and followed her into a new one.

✝

The soft rap on the door brought us out of our light sleep. Syl and Darla poked their heads into the bedroom, as I pulled the covers over our naked bodies. Maya didn't seem too disturbed with them seeing us in our birthday suits. I apparently had a bit more modesty.

"We waited until the pulsating aura around the house diminished. You should have seen what a vibrant display of lights your lovemaking emitted. It was glorious," Darla said.

I blushed profusely at the matter of fact way she had described my spiritual experience with Maya.

Maya stretched. "Finally, we were able to come together. Frankly, I was surprised that we had so much power as a match before the final culmination of our love. Good thing, huh?"

"I knew you could do it without your joining together. I don't think it would have been a success with anyone else, but you two are very special. It's why things turned out exactly as I knew they would," Darla said.

"I never quite lost hope, even when it looked like Heaven would not find her way back." Maya turned and stroked my arm.

"Twenty-four hours is usually the edge of the point of no return." Darla frowned.

"I missed a whole day," I gasped.

Maya looked at me somberly. "Now you know why I was so worried."

"I guess it makes sense why Leah wasn't still here when I woke up. You stayed by me the whole time, didn't you?"

"Of course I did. Darla and Syl came and took Leah to the main building. We knew that you had been able to ease her pain and remove the darkness, but I thought the evil had penetrated a new host—you."

"The fucker tried its best, but you were there telling me to look for the light and…" I smiled. "And then you said, 'I love you,' and I found my way to your open arms."

"Love always prevails over hate. Why don't the two of you get dressed and join us for a celebration feast?" Syl asked.

"Do we have to eat with the men?" Maya frowned.

Darla laughed. "Now, Maya, I never knew you were such an elitist. There is nothing wrong with being a heterosexual. Don't worry, we sent them on their merry way. Beanie and Gretchen may have managed to implant something inside their minds to keep them from ever returning."

"Good," Maya answered.

Leah was still not my favorite person. I thought she was fundamentally a pretentious, power-hungry individual. Someone I would never completely trust. I wanted to make sure there weren't any residual effects from what her father and Spartan had done to her. "Um…"

"Yes, we can check on Leah. She isn't as bad as you make her out to be. I think you managed to turn a lion into a pussy-cat."

I frowned but followed her as we exited our house.

†

Leah sat in the garden, looking out at the trees. She seemed at peace, but I could feel her regret and sadness. She turned her head, and her lips curled into a smile.

"No wonder Maya was always meant to surpass me. The two of you are truly glowing. I owe my life to you, Heaven. I am so sorry for whatever part I played…"

I sat next to her, and Maya joined me on the stone bench. There was just enough room for the three of us. I patted Leah's hand. "It's okay. I think everything happens for a reason. If you hadn't met Syl, I might never have met Maya. It's all good."

"You're far more forgiving than I deserve. Maybe someday I'll meet my yang and she'll help me be a better person. For so many years, the only thing driving me was my need to destroy my father. Now that he's gone, I have no purpose."

"Sure you do," I said. It flashed before me that Leah could be a wonderful mentor to the young girls who might decide to stay at the Dream Seekers' Commune.

"Like what?" she asked.

"I'm pretty sure they're going to need teachers and mentors. People who will help these kids use their gifts for good, versus evil."

"Maya's always been better at that than I have. She has more patience."

I grabbed Maya's hand and brought it to my lips. "I have plans over the next six months with Maya. I think we both have earned the time off, don't you?"

Leah's smile was genuine. "Yes, you definitely have."

†

The atmosphere in the great hall was festive. There were so many parts to this complex that I'd not seen before, including the great hall and the medical facility where some of the young girls were still recovering. A few of the others stood shyly in the corner, and I remembered what it felt like at their age and the trauma of being a lab rat. Some of them were paired, feeding off the energy of the other, as they politely watched the grown-ups make asses of themselves with too much wine, beer, and cider.

I walked over to a small, blonde girl huddled in the corner, and I felt the waves of her loneliness. When I approached the girl in isolation from everyone else, Maya gave me a nod of gratitude and I thought I saw a glint of pride in her expression.

"Hey there. My name's Heaven, what's yours?"

Her soft brown eyes blinked, and she looked at me with awe. It was very unsettling.

"You're her? You're Heaven?" she exclaimed.

"Um, yeah. And you are?"

"Forrest," she replied.

"How come you're all by yourself in the corner?" I asked.

A tear leaked out, and she mumbled, "They wouldn't let me stay with my yin. She might not make it. They were especially hard on her, because she had so much potential."

I nodded in understanding. "I know it's hard, but isolation and conjuring up strippers is not the answer."

She looked at me incredulously. "I never conjured up a stripper. Maybe a few kittens, here and there. They teased me about turning into a crazy cat lady when I grow up."

I laughed. "Sorry, I guess strippers is—was my thing."

"You have Maya, she's like…" Forrest got a dreamy look in her eyes.

"Hey now, no fantasizing about my yang! Come on, you'll hang with us until—what's your yin's name?"

"Rain," she answered.

"That's perfect. Well then, until Rain recovers, we'll be the Three Musketeers."

Forrest seemed to perk up and followed me over to Maya, who was laughing with Gretchen, who'd had a bit too much ale and was telling raucous jokes.

"You two need to clean it up, because, um…"

"Seriously?" Gretchen asked. "I'll bet Forrest has some whoppers of her own."

She grinned. "I do. Wanna hear them?"

A bunch of Weavers broke into song, and I knew it was going to be a long night with painful hangovers the next day for all.

> What shall we do with a drunken Weaver, what shall we do with a drunken Weaver, what shall we do with a drunken Weaver, early in her dream state, tie her up and make it nasty, tickle her crotch and kiss her pussy…

I tried to tug on Forrest and Maya's hands, dragging them away from the cheery revelers. They joined in the singing, along with Leah of all people, so I tossed in the towel and learned the song.

CHAPTER TWENTY-SIX

Six months later, I was not feeling the bliss. I groaned as I turned over. Maya was standing next to the bed, grinning at me. "Come on Heaven, it's uppy, uppy, time."

"Do you have to be so cheerful in the morning?"

"Yup. Do you know what day it is today?"

I did know what day it was, but I was trying to stuff that little bit of knowledge back into my subconscious. "Unfortunately, yes. Why can't I conjure up a winged creature to scoop us both up?"

"Because that would defeat the purpose of the adventure." Maya went into our small shower.

"It's not really my idea of a fun time. I can't believe I agreed to it," I grumbled. "You took advantage of me in a weakened state. Damn talented tongue," I added.

I heard the tinkling of laughter from inside the shower stall. She poked her head out. "Such a grumpy goose. I thought we'd expunged that from you."

"You can't fundamentally change who a person is," I tossed back at her. "Besides, Leah agrees with me. This is a stupid idea," I grumbled loud enough for her to hear.

"Since when do you listen to my older, but not wiser, sister?" Maya asked. "I didn't realize you two had become so close."

"She's not so bad. I suppose she kinda grows on you. She's a lot more tolerable to be around since she met Paris."

"Yeah, love will do that to you." When she stepped out fully naked and crooked her finger at me, any resistance I had went out the window. "Come on baby, it's shower time. You know how much you like to play in the water with me."

She had a point. I did love to conserve water. She'd taught me to love the basic elements of being green. I was already naked, because I didn't enjoy the restriction of clothes in the middle of the night, even though I quite enjoyed Maya's method of undressing me.

I stepped into the tiny space that wasn't exactly designed for two, but we made it work. Maya's magic fingers began a massage under my hair and made a few trips down under to my other patch of hair. The wetness of the shower wasn't the only moisture that sprung to life.

†

My leg was bouncing up and down almost in rhythm with the deep rumbling of the plane's engine. To state that I was nervous was a gargantuan understatement. I was seriously questioning not only my good sense, but the wisdom of my partners in this insanity.

Forrest and Rain were sitting across from us, and they were actually grinning.

"This is going to be so awesome," Forrest yelled over the loud noise of the flying tin can we were in.

Rain gave us a thumbs up gesture. She'd recovered nicely, even though it had been touch and go with her for a while. After Maya and I experimented with our combined power, we'd discovered an affinity for the healing arts. Even though I didn't understand exactly how it worked, it did. When Syl tried to explain everything, I gave her *the look*. She shook her head but shut up and ceased giving me the technical description of how energy flowed from one entity to another. Mumbo jumbo is what I called it, and Maya had smacked me for being so disrespectful to our gifts. I felt bad for a nanosecond.

"Woo hoo," Maya answered with gusto.

"How about I sit this one out and meet y'all on the ground?" I offered. *Am I the only one who thinks this whole idea is completely preposterous? Yup, I am. I can't understand, after barely escaping the jaws of death or worse, why they think jumping out of an airplane, voluntarily, is a good fucking idea.*

Maya got that pouty look that always caused me to back the train up and do whatever the hell she wanted me to. I was putty in her hands when she stuck out that luscious lip. "You promised."

"Again, should I remind you of the unfair tactic you chose?"

"But it's on my bucket list, and it wouldn't be the same without you. Come on, we took the safety class. It'll be a piece of cake."

"That was like thirty seconds of instruction, and some smelly guy will be wrapped in back of me instead of you," I whined.

The lead instructor came over and announced to our group, "Okay ladies, it's almost time. Are you ready?"

Everyone else screamed, "Yeah," but me. Maya grabbed one of the straps in the plane and jostled her way over to whisper in the instructor's ear. At first, he shook his head. Whatever she'd asked was a big fat no, but then his face relaxed and he nodded.

I narrowed my gaze at her, because I knew she'd entered his mind and done a little manipulation. I wondered what she was up to.

"What was that all about?" I shouted over the din inside the plane.

"We'll be doing the tandem jump together," she nonchalantly responded.

"Are you out of your fucking mind?" I shouted. "You aren't a trained professional."

"How hard can it be? I paid very close attention to all thirty seconds of his instructions. Besides, I thought this was what you wanted?"

I looked at her with total disbelief. Maya grabbed my hands, pulled me to my feet, and turned me around. I felt Maya clipping me to her body, and before I knew it, we were at the opening in the plane. The blue sky whizzed by us, reminding me we were thousands of feet in the air. I felt a gentle push, and suddenly we were flying through the air.

"I love you, Heaven—to affinity and beyond. Isn't this glorious?" she said in my ear.

The air flowed around us as we surfed the wind, and I had to admit it was exhilarating to descend from the heavens with my hands clasped tightly in Maya's. I felt myself start to relax, as an influx of calming energy seeped inside my mind.

My arms extended out and I shouted, "I love you too, you crazy woman."

Before we reached the unforgiving ground, Maya activated our parachutes and our descent slowed. I braced myself for impact, and we both managed to land without injury. Maya unclipped us and spun me around, planting a big kiss on my lips. "Ooh that was so much fun! Let's do it again, or—"

I pressed my lips onto hers before she got the chance to suggest that we bungee jump, swim with the great white sharks, climb Mt. Everest, or any other host of thrill-seeking activities she had on her bucket list. I went for something I considered reasonably tame. "I could be convinced to go up in a hot air balloon."

"That's my girl."

ABOUT THE AUTHOR

Annette Mori

Annette is an award-winning author, published by **Affinity Rainbow Publications**, who lives in the beautiful Pacific Northwest with her wife and their five furry kids. With twelve published novels and one Goldie Award for her fourth novel, Locked Inside, she finally feels like a real author. Annette is as much a reader as a writer and is always looking for the next lesfic novel to queue up. She came up with the One Fan at a Time tagline, because it rolled off the tongue much better than One Reader at a Time. After pondering who she was at her core, it was all about connecting to each reader on a personal level. Annette would be the first to admit she doesn't do well with the masses. If someone picks up her book and it touches them, she believes she has achieved what she wants with her writing by reaching each reader. It is who she is at her core. Drop her a line, she loves to hear from readers: annettemori0859@gmail.com.

Sign up for her mailing list: http://eepurl.com/cS3amj
Check out her blog https://annettemori0859.wordpress.com/
Visit the Affinity Rainbow Publications website for her books and many other outstanding authors: https://www.affinityebooks.com

OTHER AFFINITY BOOKS

<u>Gator Girlz</u> by Ali Spooner
In the sequel to *Diamond Dreams* Cam St. Angelo finished her freshman year on a high. Her softball career is on path and her lover, Everything seems to fall in place for Cam and Tab as the new school year and softball season take off. All too soon, unfortunate events at the home front, force Cam to leave collage and her softball dreams behind. As always, it's family first.

<u>The Tempest</u> by JM Dragon
Doctor Alana Cameron has dedicated her life to working on the family legacy, a transportation device which will change the world for everyone, called Tempest. Super soldier, Major Denise Trantor, who loyally defends Earth in any way possible, finds herself drawn into the Tempest program. Because of her military training, emotional bonding is not in her remit although she finds herself inexplicably drawn to Alana.

<u>Trusting Hearts</u> by Samantha Hicks
When successful advertising executive Carrie-Ann Stedman is tasked to train a new hire, she is reluctant. She has never forgiven Holly Fletcher, the newbie, for stealing an important client away from her. Holly doesn't know what Carrie's problem with her is. When the two are thrown together, can they build a working relationship with business getting in the way of the growing attraction between them?

<u>Free to Love</u> by Ali Spooner and Annette Mori
Captain Hillary Blythe loves sailing the ocean. Her journeys along the Atlantic Coast and Caribbean to deliver goods contain many adventures. When she brings a small group of rescued Africans to the Methodist mission on Antigua, challenges to deeply ingrained beliefs arise when devoted Christian, Elizabeth Allen, is drawn to one of the women—Kia. Will Kia and Elizabeth be free to love among the harsh laws of the land and Elizabeth's struggles with her faith?

<u>Kai's Heart</u> by Renee MacKenzie
The time has come for the Resistance to take back control of New America from the Anointed tyrants. Growing up as the daughter of a Resistance Army General, Kai Brodie's focus is keenly on the upcoming Revolution. So how is it then that she can't take her eyes off the beautiful Anointed guard? Can Kai break free from tradition and find love in the arms of someone her upbringing tells her she should hate? Can she protect her love from those who hunt them? Will Kai and Rachel survive the battle over the fate of their beloved New America?

<u>Diamond Dreams</u> by Ali Spooner
Cameron St. Angelo dreams of playing softball in the College World Series. Earning a scholarship to play ball for her beloved LSU brings Cam one step closer to achieving this dream. When Cam arrives on campus, she joins a family of women who share her love of the sport, and she realizes there is room in her life for another love.

<u>Unconventional Lovers</u> by Annette Mori
Bri and Siera are young women with huge hearts and strong wills; they want nothing more than to find a peaceful and secure space to be themselves. But the world is a harsh place for anyone who is different. Bri's Aunt Olivia is a vet who channels her emotions into her work and her love of Bri. Siera has her Aunt Deb who adores her. Despite their individual battles against hurt, prejudice and rejection, can these four women find love against the odds?

<u>Say You Won't Go</u> by JM Dragon & Erin O'Reilly
Logan Perry spent part of an inheritance traveling to various states, unconsciously looking for something to focus her life on. Taryn Donovan has no self-esteem and hates the waitressing job that barely keeps her in food. Can an unexpected weekend encounter turn out to be something more fulfilling? Find out in this sexually charged romance.

<u>Playing with Matches</u> by Lacey Schmidt
Dr. Augusta Stuart has devoted her adult life to supporting the mental health of disadvantaged children and moves to a new clinic in San Antonio. Her friend sets her up on a date with Callia Alexana. Prickly debates are somehow as

unexpectedly fascinating as playing with matches, and Gus is forced to consider what preconceptions she is willing to burn to find true love.

Changing Perspectives by Jen Silver
Art director, Dani Barker, lives life on the edge and finance director Camila Callaghan thinks it's necessary to stay in the closet to maintain her position. When Dani and Camila meet, they both sense an attraction, A change of perspective for both women is needed if they are to act on it.

Death is Only the Beginning by JM Dragon
What would you do if you were in a fatal accident with a stranger and ended up in heaven with them? Only to find out it wasn't an accident, it was murder. Follow the ghostly adventures of these two acrimonious strangers, who help two women find love and find closure for their predicament.

For the Love of a Woman by S. Anne Gardner
Enter a world where oil is supreme, passion rules reason and there is always the threat of civil war. In this jungle of power Raisa Andieta resides as one of its masters. Her only desire is to rule it alone. Carolyn Stenbeck is just trying to keep her marriage together. Her only desire is to be able to escape and never look back. When Raisa and Carolyn meet, it is like fuel and fire…a storm is brewing. Civil War is in the air, and passion like the coming storm begins to erupt.

The Bee Charmer by Ali Spooner

After the death of her father, Nat St. Croix needs to decide on which direction her life should take. Does she continue her life alone, as a trapper and trader, or does she start over and try to fit into a town surrounded by strangers? Will the call of the wild and all that is familiar win out, or will the call of love capture Nat's heart?

<u>The Organization</u> by Annette Mori & Erin O'Reilly
The feisty, fiery women from Asset Management are back for another heart-stopping adventure! This time, their sights are set on a new mob boss, Leonid Petrov. Val is tagged as the go-to member to infiltrate Leonid's inner circle. Tasked with keeping Leonid's impossible new wife, Gina, safe, Val encounters more problems than solutions. Will wild card Gina be Val's Achilles heel and lead to her demise, or will it fill her with a strength she didn't know she had?

<u>Running from Love</u> by Jen Silver
Sam Wade returns home from a business trip to discover her wife, Beth, has left her for another woman, Lydia. To take her mind off the breakup, Sam accepts an assignment to learn to play golf at the newly opened Temperley Cliffs Golf Resort in Cornwall, not knowing that is where Beth and Lydia plan to go too. There is more than one way to run from love; from never having to make a commitment and say those magical three words, "I love you." Find out what happens when they find themselves together—sport, betrayal, jealousy, and love form an unforgettable fusion of emotions.

eBooks, Print, Free eBooks

Visit our website for more publications available online.

www.affinityrainbowpublications.com

Published by Affinity Rainbow Publications
A Division of Affinity eBook Press NZ LTD
Canterbury, New Zealand

Registered Company 2517228

www.ingramcontent.com/pod-product-compliance
Lightning Source LLC
Chambersburg PA
CBHW051555030726
47592CB00001B/295